Kiss & Break Up

An Across the Hall Novella - Book 3

AJ Claremont

www.ajclaremont.com

Edited by Alysha Thornton @athorntonedits
Cover Design: 100covers.com

First Edition: 2026

Contents

To Lindsay, Toni, Stephanie, Erin, Emily and Erin
—everyone deserves a girl gang who shows up like you all do

Chapter 1
Harper

Fuck work, fuck this fucking job, and fuck Milo for thinking I can't do this on my own. In fact—fuck all men.

I shoot the whiskey Frankie, the bartender, just filled and slam the glass down on the sticky bar with a little more force than needed. Frankie quirks a brow.

Except Frankie. He's cool. Frankie is actively helping me get drunk.

I don't really mean fuck Milo either. He's my best friend and business partner, and he already knows everything about me, including how to put up with all my shit. He's been my ride-or-die since we ditched toxic corporate hospitality to build something better together.

He's the only person I trust with both my career and my secrets.

Which is exactly why he should have known better than to hire me an assistant. Another man thinking he knows what's best for me. I know he means well. He always does. But fuck him for thinking I need a goddamn assistant. He doesn't have one.

Because I have boundaries, Harper, he'd said. Translation: he can leave the office at a decent hour and I can't. So clearly I need someone to do my job for me. So he hired some imbecile to what...get me coffee and make photocopies or some bullshit? It's 2026. We don't even *need* photocopies. What is this kid going to do besides follow me around all day and get in my way?

I work better alone.

I throw back the rest of the whiskey and lift my hand to Frankie for a refill. Then squint at Milo's text from earlier with the name and resume of whoever this guy is.

Sullivan M. Bennett.

I don't bother opening the attachment Milo sent. I don't need to. Who names their kid Sullivan anyway?

My head is starting to throb, but I'm not quite ready to sulk back to my apartment. It's only 11 p.m. That would be the earliest I've been home in months, all because Milo said that if I didn't leave the office, he'd have his husband Parker, who's built like a linebacker, come and physically carry me home.

So I left.

Not because he told me to.

But because I wanted to stop at Bar None.

"Whiskey, neat," a voice says beside me.

I hadn't noticed anyone take the barstool next to mine. Certainly not anyone with a voice like caramel, or tiny flecks of stubble shadowing an angular jaw.

He catches me staring and lifts his glass, tipping his chin in a silent toast before taking a sip.

I don't raise my glass, but I drink anyway, eyes forward.

"Celebrating?" he asks, "or commiserating?"

The question is casual. The voice is not.

It slides low in my belly and settles there, unexpected and entirely distracting.

"Sorry," he says, pushing up from the bar. "I didn't mean that to be weird. I'll leave you to it."

He picks up his glass and wipes at a ring of condensation on the bar with his cocktail napkin before turning away without a backward glance.

"Maybe both," I say. There's something that makes me want him to stay. And before my brain catches up with my mouth, I add, "You don't have to go."

He turns back with a sheepish smile, avoiding my eyes. His hair, a warm brown, is messy in a way that looks unintentional, and the laugh lines around his eyes suggest he's older than me, but not by much. He sets his whiskey glass down on the bar but doesn't let go of it. Doesn't sit. When he finally looks at me, his eyes are warm, a deep shade of amber—but there's a hint of something underneath. Concern, maybe. Like he's bracing for something he didn't plan on.

"What about you?" I gesture to the barstool beside me. "Celebrating or commiserating?"

I don't hit on men in bars. Hell, I don't even talk to men in bars. I've learned that one polite hello can turn into a man bun explaining the weather to me or a tech bro telling me I should smile more.

But something about this guy makes me want to—I don't know.

Talk.

"Maybe both," he echoes, his tentative smile tilting a little.

And that voice ripples straight down my spine.

I'm suddenly thinking about more than conversation.

"So what are you celebrating or commiserating?" he asks, dragging my attention away from the way his forearm flexes when he swirls his whiskey glass.

"Oh," I hesitate. I'm celebrating Milo and I securing our largest client project to date, and I'm commiserating that he doesn't think I can handle it alone. But I don't want to talk about work right now. I talk about and think about work twenty-three and a half hours a day. It's usually the only thing that holds my attention.

"Just work," I finish.

Except right now.

I meet his eyes. "What about you?"

"I agreed to do a favor for an old friend," he says, sliding onto the stool.

"That's nice of you." My body angles toward his like a magnet. "I'm sure your friend appreciates it."

"He does," he says, finishing his drink in one gulp, "I'm just a little unsure if I'm up for it, you know."

His words feel broken somehow. Lived in. I take the last sip of my drink and wave to Frankie.

"You can put them both on my tab, Frankie," I say as the bartender refills our glasses. "We're celebrating."

"Congratulations," Frankie says, finishing his pour with the disinterest of a bartender who has seen too much.

"To drowning our sorrows and better tomorrows," I toast with my dad's favorite saying, and he clinks my glass with a slight chuckle. We both take long sips of our whiskey, and the alcohol, or maybe his gentle smile, loosens a knot inside my chest that I had presumed was necessary for my body to operate.

He watches me over the rim of his glass. "Bad day?"

"Bad day," I confirm. "You?"

"Bad year," he says, and there's something in his voice that makes me look closer. "Figured whiskey and people-watching might help."

"Is it helping?"

"Yeah," he says, meeting my eyes. "Actually, it is."

We fall into easy conversation after that. Not first date bullshit, but like we are on our twelfth date or twelve hundredth, like we already know all the little details, and now it's just stories and half-finished thoughts. Connection and laughter that sneaks up on me, relief of not being Harper-who-has-it-all-handled for once. Time slides by, marked only by empty glasses and the way I keep leaning a little closer without meaning to.

"Hey," he says eventually. "I have to use the restroom." He hitches a thumb over his shoulder, then hesitates. "Will you still be here, or do you need to head out?"

"No," I laugh. "It's way too early for me to go home. The neighbors wouldn't know what to think if I showed up before midnight."

"Ah." He nods, and I have the sudden, irrational urge to swim in the warm gold of his eyes when he smiles. "I used to be a night owl, too, but this is the latest I've stayed up in months."

"Maybe I should let you get to bed." And I'm pretty sure I'm smirking.

He goes quiet for a beat, studying me—or maybe choosing his next words. I hold my breath.

I don't want him to go.

"This has been well worth ruining my sleep score on my RootDown app."

Heat rushes up my neck. It's the way he's looking at me, appreciation edged with something darker, something that slides down my spine like melted chocolate.

"My business partner is obsessed with that app too," I say, forcing a lightness to my voice. "Go." I tip my chin toward the back hallway. "I'll order us another round."

He hesitates, then smiles before heading off.

I flag Frankie down, order another whiskey I absolutely don't need, and tell myself I should absolutely stay seated right here on my barstool.

That I should let this be a pleasant conversation and nothing more.

But my feet are already heading toward the bathroom hall.

When he steps out of the bathroom, he startles at the sight of me leaning against the opposite wall.

He recovers quickly, holding the door open behind him. My heart is hammering hard enough that I'm sure he can hear it echoing down the narrow hallway.

For half a second, I think about walking past him. Splashing cold water on my face. Resetting. But my head—usually crowded with deadlines and menu tests and overhead projections—won't think about anything but him.

I hook my finger into his belt loop and tug.

He looks down, confused for exactly one beat, then lets me guide him backward into the small bathroom. I reach behind him to twist the lock, the click loud in the quiet space. I'm close enough to feel the heat of him, close enough to hear when his breath hitches.

"I've never really..." he pauses, swallows. "I don't usually—"

I quiet him with my mouth.

His lips are warm and taste like whiskey—his or mine, I can't tell—and his hand slides around my waist. I deepen the kiss, and he responds immediately, stepping closer, backing me up until the counter digs into my hip.

"You taste incredible." He kisses down my neck to my exposed collarbone. I rise on my toes to give him better access. He hoists me onto the counter and steps between my legs, my skirt hiking up, exposing bare thighs, He lets out an appreciative sigh.

I twist my hands in his shirt and drag him closer. His chest is solid beneath my fingertips, his pulse pounding hard and fast, matching mine. We kiss until my lips feel bruised, but it's not enough. I reach for the button of his jeans, and he pulls back, just a millimeter from my lips.

"I live close by, do you want to—" he starts, then his mouth finds mine again. His hands slide up my thighs, thumbs pressing into the inside of my legs, close enough to send sparks across my skin, but not close enough.

I live nearby, too. A few blocks. But I'm already too close to combustion to leave. Besides, if we stop now, I might come to my senses. Start thinking.

And right now, I don't want the part of my brain that runs ten steps ahead, calculating outcomes and spotting missteps. I want the small, neglected part that just wants to feel good. To focus on his hand gripping my thigh, almost possessively, while the other slips beneath my sweater for the first time.

"I don't want to leave," I breathe when his thumb grazes my nipple. "I want this. Now."

"God, you feel incredible," he murmurs against my neck as his hand slides up my thigh. His grip is firm, thumbs digging into my legs, close enough to make me ache. "I want to touch you more."

"Do it." I rock my hips forward to meet his hand.

His thumb drags upward, and he lets out a breathless curse when he realizes how wet I am for him.

"Yes," I gasp, pulling his mouth back to mine as his thumb slips beneath the elastic of my underwear. He strokes slowly at first, then with purpose, until he finds a rhythm that makes my whole body tense. I writhe against the counter as he circles my clit with steady, deliberate pressure, and I can feel myself tightening almost immediately.

"That's right, sweetheart."

When I'm about to beg for more, he slides two fingers inside me.

The sensation is shocking and exactly what I want, and I shatter. My breath catches as the orgasm crashes through me, fast and overwhelming, my body convulsing as it takes over completely. He doesn't pull away. He keeps the same rhythm, guiding me through with soft praises—*that's right, I've got you*—until I'm trembling and boneless against him.

I can't speak. I can barely move. But I need my mouth on his again.

"I'm Max," he stammers between my desperate kisses. "I never—we never—"

I fumble for his zipper, desperate to touch him now.

"Fuck," he groans when I slide my hand into his jeans. He's already hard. I squeeze him once, desperate to feel more of him.

"Do you have a condom?" I say, scooting to the edge of the counter.

"Oh. Yeah. I think—" he grits out, my hand moving rougher now. "But do you—are you sure?"

The familiar buzz of my phone makes my hand falter. He stills.

"Shit." I pull my hand free, and reality slams back.

"It's okay," he rushes. "I'm sorry. We don't have to do anything."

"No," I say, hopping down from the counter and reaching for my bag. "You were great." The words come out distracted, my head still spinning from whiskey and aftershocks of my orgasm as I dig my phone out of my tote. "Shit," I say again when I see the screen.

I look up to find him watching me. Max—was that his name?—breathing hard, his fly still undone.

His expression is a mix of uncertainty and something darker. Something helpless, and somehow almost demanding.

I wanted to linger. To sink back into the kiss. To let this moment stretch into something more.

But everyone was counting on me. Milo. Jessica. Kincade. I can't let myself get distracted by a stranger in a bar bathroom.

Especially not by the confusing pull of not wanting him to stay a stranger.

"Look..." I start, not sure what I'm even about to say.

For a dizzying second, I consider staying.

I could take this call, talk Kincade off whatever ledge he's on, then walk back to my place with Max. Finish this in an actual bed. Maybe grab coffee in the morning. Find out what made him have a bad year.

What am I doing?

I'm in a dive bar bathroom, not a Hallmark movie.

My phone buzzes again. I have to take this call, even though it's well past midnight. I need to stay focused on what matters.

This can't matter.

I need to leave. Alone.

"Look," I say, forcing a detached smile. "This was great. Really. Thank you." I lean up and press one last kiss to his mouth. "But I have to go."

I slip out of the bathroom and pull the door closed behind me, smoothing my skirt as I head for the exit.

"Close me out, Frankie!" I call over my shoulder. "Add twenty for you!"

"Okay, Harper," he answers with a wave. "See you next time."

I reach the front door and pause. Some reckless part of me hopes the handsome stranger will follow me.

He doesn't.

Good.

It's better this way.

At least that's what I tell myself as I step out into the cool midnight air.

Chapter 2
Max

I sit on my board and match my breathing to the steady rise and fall of the ocean, the horizon still pale with morning. My therapist's voice threads through my head, steady and annoying in the way things are when advice you didn't want to take is working.

Five things I can see: The sun just breaking over the water. The dark line of the shore. A gull skimming low across the surface. The scratches on the nose of my board. The slow rise of the swell beneath me.

Four things I can feel: The board under me. The cold seep of the Pacific through my wetsuit. The tight pull in my shoulders from paddling too frantically at first. The steady thump of my heart, slowing.

Three things I can hear: Water lapping against fiberglass. The distant crash of a wave breaking. My own breath, even and measured.

Two things I can smell: Salt air. Neoprene.

One thing I can taste: Her.

The faint memory of whiskey and her lips lingers longer than it has any right to.

And I didn't get enough.

Not that she owes me anything. She doesn't. The memory of her coming apart around my fingers could go to my grave with me as one of the best moments of my life. But it wasn't enough.

I wanted more.

I want it again—the sharp little gasp she made, the way those green eyes found mine when I touched her, the way her hand tightened in my hair, the brief sting as she pulled just hard enough. The way her body craved mine, leaning in, pulling closer. The way it convulsed when she finally let go.

And then her damn phone rang.

She didn't silence it.

Didn't ignore it.

Didn't toss it into the toilet the way I silently begged her.

She answered it.

With my fingers still slick with her.

She slid off the counter, smoothed her skirt, and kissed me with the phone still pressed to her ear. And before I could process what was happening, before I could stop her, she was gone, disappearing out of the bathroom like maybe she did that all the time.

I didn't even get her name.

What was I thinking? I flew across the country to focus on work. Just work. To rebuild my career without losing myself this time.

This was supposed to be controlled. Safe. A test to see if I can dip my toe back in without letting it swallow me whole. To see if everything from the last year and a half actually stuck. The therapy, the affirmations, the slow work of figuring out how I broke and how to put myself back together.

Not to complicate things with a beautiful stranger who makes me want to break my own rules.

A set rolls in on the horizon, darker water lifting in a slow, deliberate line. I feel it before I really see it, the ocean drawing a breath. It's a good wave. Maybe more than one. The kind I would normally turn and paddle for without hesitation.

But I stay where I am, just beyond the break, letting it pass beneath me.

Since I started surfing again, this part has become as important as—maybe more than— catching the perfect wave. Learning patience. Learning that not every opportunity needs to be seized, not every swell chased. That disappointment doesn't mean failure.

That's what I'm supposed to be focused on. The steps of my recovery. Not letting old patterns dress themselves up as something new. Last night was impulsive. Exactly the kind of thing I'm supposed to avoid. I'm supposed to take three deep breaths before I say yes to anything.

But when she pressed her mouth to mine, or maybe when she tugged me into the bathroom, or hell, when she invited me to sit back down on the barstool, I knew I'd say yes to whatever she asked.

And that's the problem.

That's what got me here in the first place.

Why don't you feel like you can say no, Max? My therapist had asked during one of my first sessions—back when I was still bitter and angry and raw.

Because you don't get to the top by saying no.

You get there by being the one who always says yes.

The job. The marriage. Both required me to say yes to everything and no to myself. It worked—right up until it broke me.

I hold my fist up to the thin strip of sky between the horizon and the newly risen sun. 6 a.m.

I should head in. Shower. Get dressed.

Even if it's just a favor for an old friend.

Even if it's only three months.

Even if it's nowhere near the level of what I used to do.

Not every swell needs to be chased.

I turn my board toward shore, already feeling the familiar pull of routine settling back into place.

I should be on time for my first day at my new job.
That's what matters.

Chapter 3
Harper

"You look like shit," Milo says, glancing up from the architectural renderings spread across the front table as I walk in.

I glance at my phone. Milo is never here before I am. But it's 8:07—I'm never this late. But I slept like shit, so no surprise I look like it too.

"Yeah, well, being told by your business partner that you can't do your job will do that to a girl." Saccharine sarcasm coating my voice as I drop my bag onto our office manager Jessica's desk.

"My guess is," Milo says, circling the table and waving a finger at me, "you exceeded your rule of no more than two top-shelf whiskeys, and put them all on the company credit card while cursing me, this job, and all of mankind."

"Not all of mankind," I reply. "The bartender at Bar None is cool."

Milo studies me long enough that I roll my shoulders back and stand a little taller.

We run a casual office—another way Milo and I promised ourselves we'd do things differently when we started Studio Mise—but today I wore heels. Power heels, my mom used to call them. At five-eight, I'm not short, but the extra height puts me eye to eye with Milo. And any idiot teenager I might have to deal with today.

"You know I don't think you're incapable, right?" Milo says, and I know him well enough to hear the careful way he chooses his words. "I think you care too much. You take on everyone's problems. You stay late so I can go home to Parker. You restructure deals to give Jessica a bigger cut. You take the blame when things go wrong, whether it's your fault or not."

I open my mouth to argue, but he holds up a hand.

"You give everyone else what they need, Harper. I wanted to hire someone to give you what you need."

"I'm fine, Milo."

"I know you think you are." He leans forward. "But this Bites by Blake concept is a big deal. It's exactly the exposure we've been looking for. I want it to go smoothly—"

"*I'll* make it go smoothly," I snap.

"Without it costing me my best friend," he continues evenly, "or her mental health."

"Next, you're going to try to make me meditate or some shit," I say, but I'm already softening.

"I wouldn't dream of it."

"So where did you find this kid anyway?" I glance around the front office like my new assistant might be hiding behind the curtains. "Am I going to have to put him down for a nap or drive him back for his seventh-period homeroom class?"

"Harper, he's not—"

"He better not ask me to fucking prom!" I say, disappearing into my office.

I drop into my desk chair and pull up the latest spreadsheets, but the numbers blur.

I try to focus on Kincade Smith's demands—the investor behind our next project. It was his idea to hand a restaurant to a viral TikToker—Blake Adams—on the assumption that we could capitalize on his millions of views. Instead, the chaos this project has unleashed is mind-numbing.

Kincade has a talent for harebrained demands disguised as brilliant ideas.

Like his call last night.

Last night.

The thought triggers a memory of my caramel-voiced bar companion. His hands on my body. His lips on my neck. The way his fingers coaxed me apart until I forgot, briefly, how tightly I hold myself together.

I'm no stranger to a well-placed one-night stand. But last night felt different. The orgasm was incredible, yes, but it was the ease of it, the connection, the way I caught myself imagining what came *after*, that has me off-balance eight hours later.

And maybe that's why I left in such a hurry.

Or that I'm wondering what he's doing right now. Where he might be.

I shake my head and click through to the budget tab.

Sure, if Kincade hadn't called rambling about something that absolutely could have waited until morning, I probably would have let Max fish a condom from his wallet and finish what we started. But it wasn't the interruption that rattled me.

It was the thought that I would have asked him to come home with me afterward.

Something I never do.

That thought unsettles me far more than anything Kincade was yammering about.

So I left. Without Max's number or any real way for either of us to find the other again. And honestly, it's probably better that way. For both of us.

I've more or less given up on men. Or at least on the idea that they can be anything more than a means to an end. I have good friends—Milo, Amelia, and Mr. Evans. And I have good sex when I have time for it. But I gave up on wanting both in the same person a long time ago. That's a recipe for disaster.

I'm married to my job. Just like my mom was.

I'm not naive; I saw where that got her. I always thought my dad was great, and I understand he was frustrated. Mom never put him before her work. But if he couldn't live with that, he should have had the decency to divorce her first before...before moving on.

That's why I keep my worlds separate.

Friends. Sex. Work.

Three distinct buckets. No messy overlap.

So whatever happened last night stays in that bathroom. One-time thing. Done. Over.

My phone pings.

Amelia: *Did you work all weekend or actually do something fun??*

I stare at the message from my best friend, unsure how to answer. I go for distraction instead.

Harper: *It was fine. How's my Penelope?*

Amelia: *Puking all weekend. I was hoping to live vicariously through you.*

I need to choose my words carefully. We tell each other everything, so too many or too few details and Amelia will know something's up. I'm not sure what to tell her, and I'm not ready to unpack that yet.

Harper: *You know, work, my favorite neighborhood dive bar, then more work*

I leave out the part about the hottest man I've ever met rendering me boneless in the bathroom.

I glance at the time. 8:45. Fifteen minutes until Sullivan Bennett arrives—assuming he's capable of getting himself out of bed before midmorning. Milo claims he told him nine, which is already a compromise. 9 a.m. is two hours later than I like to start my day, so my new assistant is already behind, and we haven't even met yet.

I hear Jessica talking animatedly to someone in the front office.

I round my desk, pausing inside my office door.

"You must be Sullivan?" she says in her perpetually too-perky lilt.

Here we go. Let's meet the toddler.

I straighten the belt of my intentionally all-black outfit and steel myself. I've learned it's best to let people assume I'm the villain right away. Milo can be the golden retriever. I'm the black cat.

"Oh, here's Ms. Wells now," Jessica chirps as I step out. "Harper, this is Sullivan."

"Benster!" Milo booms from his office down the hall.

"Harper?"

That voice—confused, warm, and unmistakably caramel-soft—stops me cold.

"Max?" I choke.

"No, Sullivan," Jessica corrects brightly.

"Benny, Ben, Benster," Milo continues, appearing behind us.

My head whips toward him.

"You're Harper?" Max asks again, pulling my attention back to his eyes. Those same amber pools I got lost in last night.

"Yes," Jessica says. "This is Harper Wells, your new boss."

My stomach drops.

"Benny, I'm so glad you're here," Milo sings, utterly oblivious to the emotional car crash unfolding in front of him.

"Why are you calling him *Benny*?" I snap, my irritation ricocheting in every direction at once.

"That's what we called him back in our Beta Kappa days."

"You were in a fraternity?" Jessica asks, delighted.

"Yeah," Milo shrugs. "Back when I was pretending to be straight."

"Why did you tell me your name was Max?" I demand, turning back to him.

"Wait—you've met?" Milo's eyes bounce between us like he's watching a tennis match.

"That's what I go by," Max says tightly. "Why didn't you tell me you were Harper?"

"I did."

"No, you didn't. Or I would have never—"

"Never what?" Milo asks.

"Nothing!" Max and I shout in perfect, horrifying unison.

The room goes silent. My heart hammers so loudly I'm sure everyone can hear it.

"Okay," Jessica says after a beat, glancing down at her clipboard. "So you go by Max?"

"Yeah. It's my middle name." He doesn't take his glare off me.

Sullivan M. Bennett.

"It's on my résumé," he adds, clipped. And it's clearly directed at me.

"Oh! You're right." Jessica nods, scribbling. "Preferred name: Max. Not a problem. All your forms still have your full legal name."

"What kind of name is Sullivan?" I quip, not entirely sure why.

"You didn't seem concerned about my name last night," he says—low enough that only I hear.

"Okay!" Milo says, his eyes flicking warily between us. "Sullivan Maxwell Bennett, this is my business partner, Harper Eloise Wells. I don't have a middle name, but I like to pretend it's Prince."

"Could you sign here, Sull—Max," Jessica says, thrusting the clipboard at him.

He takes it without breaking eye contact with me. His jaw is tight, a muscle ticking beneath his cheekbone.

And while I'm not one to back down from confrontation, I suddenly have somewhere I need to be. Anywhere but here. I don't need an assistant. And I definitely don't need one whose hands were on my—

"I need to go," I snap, grabbing my bag. "Jessica will—" What? Show him around? Set up a desk for him in my office so I have to sit five feet from him and somehow ignore the way his voice does unforgettable things to my insides? I can't think. "Milo will get you settled out here."

And then I walk out of the office.

I'm not sure where I'm going.

Only that I cannot stay here.

Chapter 4

Max

I've never had a one-night stand. I don't sleep with someone on the first date. Hell, Melanie and I dated for half a semester before we had sex. I liked knowing a person first. Liked believing that connection made everything better.

And yet I felt more connection with Harper last night—over whiskey and half-finished stories, in a dive bar bathroom with my hands on her body and my heart somehow already in her palm—than I'd had with anyone else in years.

And now, for the second time in less than twelve hours, I'm watching her walk away from me.

"Sorry, man," Milo says, his mouth pulling into an embarrassed grimace. "That had way more to do with me than with you."

"Yeah," I say, still watching the door like she might come back. "Should I maybe go?"

Milo snorts softly. "Nah, she's dramatic when she's overwhelmed," he says. "And right now? She's overwhelmed." Suddenly, his eyes go wide. "Never tell her I said she's overwhelmed."

"This is not comforting."

"She'll come around," he says, clapping me on the shoulder. "Harper's just...intense. But she's brilliant. You'll see."

Intense. Brilliant. Married to her work.

I've been here before.

And I told myself I wouldn't do it again.

Melanie used to take calls during dinner. During date nights. Once during a funeral.

But I was like that, too. We both were. We'd work sixteen-hour days and call it dedication. Cancel plans and call it ambition. We understood each other because we were the same.

Until I wasn't anymore.

"She thinks my saying we could use an extra set of hands on this huge restaurant project is a direct attack on her." Milo's easy air fades, replaced by something more serious. "But it's not because I think she can't do it. It's because I know she will. At all costs. And I care about her too much to watch her drive herself into the ground for this." He looks at me. "You understand that, right?"

I do. Maybe more than Milo realizes.

I told him a little about why I wasn't at the firm anymore. That I didn't want the pace. That I needed time to regroup. I didn't tell him about waking up in the middle of the night, drenched in sweat. Or throwing up in the trash can outside my office. Or the morning I rode the subway all the way to the end of the line because I couldn't force myself to get off at my stop.

Or how when I told Melanie I needed to slow down, needed us to slow down, she barely looked up from her laptop. And when she did, it was like I'd broken our deal. Like asking for partnership was somehow selfish.

"Look," Milo says when I don't respond. "This morning confirmed you were the help she didn't ask for. A résumé she didn't read. And apparently some off-the-clock history."

He says the last part carefully.

"We met last night," I admit. "I didn't know who she was."

"I know," Milo says, pressing a hand to his chest. "That part's on me, too." He huffs a laugh. "It also explains the larger-than-average Bar None tab on the company card. So, you bonded over a love of top-shelf whiskey?"

Among other things.

"Yeah," I say. "It was nice."

"Well," Milo says, hopeful, "then you already know Harper isn't entirely the black cat she wants everyone to think she is. She's...an Enneagram Eight."

"I don't know what that means."

"It means she's great," Milo says. "And exhausting. And allergic to feeling like she needs anyone."

I'm not sure what to make of that.

My head is spinning, and there's a dull ache in my chest I can't quite place. Milo and I lost touch after undergrad, but we'd been close once, the least fratty frat boys, bonded more by sarcasm than bravado. When I saw he'd launched a boutique restaurant consulting firm, I reached out to congratulate him.

At the time, I was bouncing between my therapist, my financial planner, and my divorce attorney. He told me he and his business partner had left the corporate hospitality grind to try to do things differently.

That part stuck.

I wanted to do things differently too.

Then he called a few weeks ago, saying his business partner needed support. And I wanted something short-term. Low-stakes. No one's livelihood riding on my decisions.

So I said yes.

I sublet my New York apartment and moved into a furnished place in the Outer Richmond with a three-month lease and a very clear end date.

Eventually, I'd have to go back to New York. Face the people who watched me unravel. Prove to them, and maybe mostly to myself, that this worked. That I'm fixed. That the breakdown wasn't the end of my career.

Three months helping an old friend. No authority. No pressure.

A clean slate.

That was the plan.

Until Harper.

Milo clears his throat. "Look. Let me handle Harper."

I glance up.

"I know where she goes to cool off," he says. "Jessica can get you settled. Show you where everything is. Take the rest of the afternoon off. We'll all take a breath and start fresh tomorrow."

"I'm not here to step on her toes," I say. "I'll stay out of her way. Do what you actually hired me for."

Milo smiles, relieved. "Backend systems. Spreadsheets. Making my life easier."

I nod. That I can do.

And I mean it.

Whatever happened last night was bad timing, worse judgment. She's my boss. And I need this to be simple.

I didn't move across the country to fall into old patterns.

Three months.

Keep my head down. Do the work. Get out.

Nothing more.

Chapter 5

Harper

I stare up the short flight of steps of the Victorian that houses Studio Mise like it is my first day of work, not Max's.

After I stormed out yesterday, Milo gave me exactly thirty-seven minutes to fume before finding me in my favorite bookstore down the street. I hated that he knew where I went when I needed to cool off. Hated that he didn't tell me to come back, didn't say I was being unreasonable, didn't tell me I was being an ass.

Instead, Milo apologized. Said he shouldn't have hired Max without talking to me first. That he never thought I needed an assistant—Max was general support for the whole team.

Give it a week. If I still felt like I didn't need him around, we'd make other arrangements.

One week. Fine.

I take a long, steadying breath and glance at my phone. 7:04. At least I'll have a few hours alone before the rest of the office arrives. Before I have to face Max, and his infuriating brown eyes, in person.

I jiggle the key in the old lock and shove the door open with my shoulder.

Max would come in at nine, leave by four, and help Jessica and Milo. I'd be on-site with Blake and Kincade most of the time anyway.

We'd barely see each other.

This would be fine.

It has to be fine.

Because I'm not doing—whatever this pull toward him is. Not the heat of that night. Not the connection that was too intense to write off as a random hook up. Not the way my chest tightened when he looked at me yesterday like I'd betrayed him. I hadn't meant to be rude, I just...don't do well with surprises. But now I'm prepared. I could do this.

Compartmentalize. Move on. Get back to work.

"Harper?"

I shriek in the entryway, my heavy tote slipping from my shoulder and spilling onto the floor.

"What the fuck," I stammer as Max hurries around Jessica's desk, crouching to gather the papers that have scattered everywhere.

"I'm so sorry—I didn't mean to scare you."

"You didn't scare me," I snap, dropping down to shove things back into my bag. "I've got it."

"Right. Sorry." He straightens and steps back, hands up in surrender.

"What are you doing here so early?" I ask, refusing to meet his eyes.

"I know Milo said the office doesn't really start until nine, but..." He pauses, and damn it, I look up.

Those eyes. Like gravity.

No.

Not doing this.

"I guess I'm still on East Coast time," he says. "Milo gave me a key, I figured I'd come in early. Get a jump on the learning curve."

"What were you even working on?"

"He asked me to familiarize myself with the budget and the project timeline," he says, rubbing the back of his neck like he's suddenly aware he's being evaluated. "I noticed everything was spread across six different spreadsheets, so I started combining them into one that's a little more accessible for the team."

Of course he did.

Of course he's competent and organized and exactly what Milo said we needed.

I hate it.

"Do you even have any restaurant experience?"

He looks at me for a beat, and for half a second I'm not in the office anymore. I'm back in that bar bathroom. His hands on my body. His breath on my neck. The way he looked at me like I was something he wanted to unravel.

"Um," a nervous laugh threads through his voice. "Other than eating at them?"

I arch a brow.

"No," he adds. "No restaurant experience."

I let out an annoyed huff.

But the truth is, I already knew that.

After I went home yesterday and took a shower with water the temperature of molten lava, I tried to look at the budget projections and couldn't focus. I crawled into bed with one of my favorite romance novels and still couldn't focus—my mind drifting, annoyingly, back to Max—I finally gave in and opened the résumé Milo had sent over days ago.

Undergrad at UC Berkeley. Magna Cum Laude.

MBA from NYU Stern.

Summer internship at Goldman.

Five years at West Financial Group, rising to junior partner by twenty-nine, focused on mergers and acquisition. Known internally for restructuring teams and processes during high-growth acquisitions.

A quick Google search filled in that two years ago, he'd landed on the *New York Times* 40 Under 40 to Watch in Finance list.

So no. He doesn't have restaurant experience.

But he has everything else.

With those qualifications, I can't understand why Milo would hire him for general office help. Or why Max would take it.

"Just do what Jessica tells you," I say, slinging my bag onto my shoulder. "She's better to learn from anyway. More patient."

I step past him toward my office.

"Harper," Max says, moving just enough to block my path. "Are we not going to talk about—"

"There's no need," I cut in. My voice is calm. Professional. But I refuse to look directly at him. "We both have jobs to do." I straighten, squaring my shoulders. "Let's agree to stay out of each other's way."

"Fine," he says, voice flat. "You got it."

"Great."

"I'm not doing this again," he mutters, more to himself than to me.

He turns and walks away, leaving me standing there like an idiot.

I storm back to my office and hide until well after eleven, when the coffee I've been mainlining all morning finally forces me out.

I've been listening to Milo's animated voice and Jessica's laughter for the past hour. Max's deep voice underlies it all—I can't make out his words, but whatever he is saying is keeping them delighted.

I round my desk but pause at the door as another burst of laughter erupts. Maybe I could stay in here until everyone leaves for lunch.

What are you doing? Harper Wells doesn't hide.

I yank open my door with more force than necessary, and all three heads swivel toward me.

"Harper!" Milo says. "Settle an argument about where to order lunch. Jessica says the best pho is the place on 8th Avenue. But I think it's that little spot behind the dry cleaners on Castro. Which place do you think Max would like more?"

Max looks at me with a hopeful smile.

"I...how would I know what he likes?" I say, though it's obviously the place on Castro. I want their jammy egg to be my last meal.

"Okay," Milo says slowly, pulling out his phone. "I'm going to order. You want the clay pot, Harps, add a jammy egg?" he asks, typing.

My mouth waters.

"No thanks. I need to get to that meeting with Spencer," I say, turning back into my office for my bag. I'll stop at the coffee shop on the corner to pee.

"I thought that wasn't until three," Jessica says.

I shoot her a look I hope translates to please don't make this harder. She just smiles back.

"I have a few stops to make first." I hoist the rolls of architectural drawings Spencer sent over to review.

"Hey." Max pushes back from his chair, then stops in front of me. We both go still, like someone hit pause. He takes a slow breath.

"I know you don't need help," he says, his voice calm and deliberate. "But if there's anything I can do that would make today easier, I'd be happy to. It's my job."

The blueprints shift in my arms, and one slips free, rolling across the table.

Max's eyes flick down.

He doesn't move. Doesn't reach for it.

He just waits.

My heart thuds once, hard. I don't know why that feels...significant.

"I could help you get these to the Uber," he adds. "If you want."

"I'll probably take a Waymo," I say, holding his gaze. "I like not having to talk to anyone."

Max's careful expression cracks with a smile.

"Fair," he says. "Then...would you like help carrying them downstairs?"

I sigh.

"Fine."

He nods like he's won an important argument.

We reach the bottom of the stairs and step out onto the sidewalk. I pull out my phone, thumb hovering over the Waymo app, then hesitate.

"I think it might be faster to walk," I say, already mentally mapping caffeine and a bathroom stop.

"Of course," Max says easily, shifting the stack of plans to hand them to me.

The rolled plans immediately start to unfurl in my arms. I try to wrangle them, nearly drop one, and end up clutching the whole mess awkwardly to my chest.

Max just watches, one eyebrow raised.

"Ugh, fine," I snap. "Could you just walk with me?"

"I'd be happy to," he says, and I swear there's a smirk tugging at his mouth.

He reaches for the plans.

"I mean," I say as our fingers brush, little sparks lighting across my skin. I quickly tip the plans into his arms and pull away. "You really need to get up to speed on this project. I could explain it on the way."

"I think that would be helpful," he says, still smiling. He motions down the street. "Lead the way."

"So," I say, taking a steadying breath when we begin walking. "What has Milo told you?"

"I want to hear everything from you," he says. "Milo is great, but I feel like you have all the details and a system of explaining things that will align with how my brain processes information."

I look up at him, a little shocked.

"Did that sound really nerdy?" he says, a faint blush across his cheekbones.

No, I think it was kind of...hot?

"Okay, stop me if this is all too basic. I know you are..." I hesitate, "qualified."

"Treat me like I'm a nineteen-year-old intern who can barely make it to work on time."

I suck in a breath. I'm going to kill Milo.

"It's fine, Harper," he laughs, and it's a sound that I feel in my chest more than hear. "I get it. I've had my share of incompetent assistants and interns. I don't blame you for having your doubts about me. But I'm taking this job seriously. This matters to me."

"For this project," I say, trying to ignore how my insides warm at his words. Why is competence so damn attractive? "We've been hired by Kincade Smith, an investor who, if I'm being honest, makes wild assumptions and takes big risks. They don't always pay off, but when they do, they are huge. He was the investor behind Tokyo House. But he's really...um...confident."

"Yeah, I've met guys like that," Max agrees.

"Are you on TikTok?"

"Not at all," Max laughs. "I'm way too old."

"You're not too old, you're like thirty-five, right?"

"Yeah, but I feel like I'm sixty-five stuck in a thirty-five-year-old's body sometimes."

My eyes dart across the bulge in his bicep where he's gripping the plans, the long line of his shoulders, the broad expanse of his chest.

My mouth goes dry.

Max glances down at me, waiting for me to go on. I swallow and continue.

"Kincade is banking on this guy who has gone mega viral on TikTok—foodtok—Blake Adams. He dropped out of culinary school and started hosting these secret pop-up dinners in LA."

"I think I heard about those," Max says. "Like you had to be on the list, then decode some sort of map to find the location, and it was always like an abandoned building or something?"

"See, you're hip with what the youngsters are doing," I joke.

"All I could think about when I heard about it was what OSHA would think about these locations...so maybe not so hip."

I laugh despite myself.

"Hey, would you mind if we stopped in here real quick?" I gesture to the coffee shop we're about to pass.

"Of course," Max says, holding the door open for me.

"I'm going to run to the restroom."

"What's your coffee order?" he asks, getting into the line.

"Oh, I can get it."

"I'm your assistant," he says. "The least I can do is get you coffee."

I huff out a short laugh. "Fine. Cappuccino. Extra shot. Extra hot." I hold out my company credit card.

He looks at it. Then at me.

"Let me get it," he says, with a shy smile.

"It's a work expense."

His jaw tightens. "Right."

He takes the card.

Good.

This isn't a date.

This is a work meeting.

"Thanks," I say, already turning toward the hallway. "I'll be right back."

I don't look at him as I head for the bathroom. I don't give myself the chance to wonder why my chest feels tight now.

I don't regret Bar None.

I don't make second-guessing my choices a habit.

But Max isn't a stranger in a bar anymore. He's a distraction.

And distractions are expensive.

Chapter 6

Max

The Studio Mise office is more casual than the firms I worked in back in New York, but the pace is surprisingly familiar.

The first week blurs together in a rush of meetings, site visits, deliveries, and me trying to keep track of the overlapping timelines, spreadsheets, and personalities involved in launching a San Francisco restaurant. Where I used to work inside massive firms with entire departments for each task, Milo, Harper, and Jessica are the departments. All of them. At once.

They operate in a kind of organized chaos, wearing every hat and never slowing down. Contractors rotate in and out. Decisions get made on the fly. And somehow, everything still moves forward.

No one works harder than Harper.

She's the first one in every day—I don't make that mistake again—and the last to leave. She shoos everyone out at five, then stays until eight. Or nine. Or later.

She keeps her head down and her door closed.

She never joins us for lunch. I never see her eat. Just coffee, like an IV drip, like she can outwork her own needs.

She barely speaks to me in person but sends clipped, precise requests to my admin@studiomise.com email, time-stamped at 10 p.m., 6 a.m., or once at three in the morning.

I'd think she was avoiding me.

Except this is just who she is.

Harper is the backbone of the company. All control, no nonsense. Someone who chooses work over everything else, every time. I've been here before. Hell, I was her before.

But that's not me. Not what I want anymore.

I came to San Francisco to rebuild. To prove I could work without losing myself. Not to make excuses for green eyes and a brilliant mind, no matter how attracted I am to both.

Whatever happened in that bar was a fluke—chemistry without context, attraction without consequence.

And I need to keep it that way.

My therapist says I have a tendency to revisit my mistakes, to replay them until they lose all proportion. She calls them "learning opportunities," like I'm a third grader who forgot his homework.

Harper Wells is a *learning* opportunity.

I'm here to practice work-life balance. To prove I can handle pressure without breaking. Clock in. Clock out. Surf. Meditate. Maintain boundaries.

I've worked too hard to let a moment in a dive bar bathroom—no matter how charged—disrupt the structure that keeps everything else standing.

"Milo!" Harper shouts from her office as I step through the front door on Friday morning.

I pause, keys still in my hand, and glance around the empty office.

"Uh," I call back. "It's Max."

There's a beat.

"Never mind," she says.

I exhale through my nose and walk down the hall anyway, nudging her half-closed door open with my knuckles.

"Is there something I can help you with, Harper?"

She looks up over the edge of her laptop. Her eyes catch on mine, long enough to register, before she drops her gaze again, like she's annoyed at me for interrupting, or annoyed at herself for noticing.

"No," she says, without looking at me, "I just need the square footage of the site for these calculations."

I shift in the doorframe. "It's nineteen hundred square feet. Kitchen's slated at five hundred. Bar's another two-fifty to three, depending on the layout."

She looks up again, pausing like she's deciding whether to comment.

"How are you walking around with those numbers in your head?" she asks.

"I read the deck," I say. "Twice."

A corner of her mouth twitches despite herself, then she tips her chin at the two coffee cups in the tray I'm holding. "What's that?"

"Coffee."

"For who?" she asks carefully.

"For you." I lift the cup from the carrier but don't offer it yet. "If you want it. Cappuccino. Extra shot. Extra hot. From Marco's."

"You remembered my order?"

"I'm your assistant," I say evenly. "It's my job to remember things."

But we both know that's not why I remembered.

"Thanks," she says. When she takes it, our fingers brush. The contact lasts half a second too long.

This was supposed to be a peace offering. A professional gesture.

Why does it feel like more?

"But you're not my assistant," she says, pulling back slightly. "You're general office help."

"Right." I step back. "Then I'll be out here doing general office stuff if you need me."

She shakes her head. "I've got it."

Of course she does. Her perfect control slides back into place.

"Did I just catch you napping?" Harper scoffs, coming from her office twenty minutes later.

I open one eye from where I'm sitting in the front window. Then close it again and inhale. "Nope, just meditating."

It's quiet, but I can tell she hasn't moved. I open my eyes again.

"Really?" she asks, almost curious.

"Yes, it's how I," I pause, "prepare to handle my day."

She lets out a little burst of laughter that feels like eating Pop Rocks candy, and I desperately want to hear it again.

"To handle me?" she asks, smirking.

Yes.

"No," I say. "It's my morning practice."

I stop short of telling her it's how I manage my anxiety. That my therapist thought it would help with my panic attacks, but now it's simply how I like to start each day.

"It's a reset," I offer. "Helps me transition from my home life to work life."

She's watching me, her red lips pressed into a line. Her black blouse has a tie at her collar that draws my eyes to the dip at her throat. I swallow and pull my gaze back up to her eyes.

"I don't think I have that," she says, still watching me.

"A transition practice?"

"Two different lives."

"It's all work," I say, and it's not a question.

She leans her hip against Jessica's desk, and I track every movement. The way she crosses her arms over her chest, her crossed ankle peeking just beneath the hem of her fitted black skirt.

I close my eyes again. Not to return to my practice, but to pull my gaze away from her.

"Does it help?" she asks. And I wonder for a moment if I did say the anxiety part out loud or if she somehow knows that's what I meant.

"It does," I say, keeping my eyes closed, inhaling deeply, hoping maybe she'll follow. "You should try it."

She laughs again, this time sharper. "I don't have time." I hear her push off the desk, her heels clicking across the hardwood floor back to her office.

"Enjoy your nap!" she calls before I hear her door click closed again.

An hour later, a sharp "Fuck!" comes from Harper's office.

She stomps out, her open laptop in hand, bending over the front table in a way that does dangerous things to her curves. "Fuck, fuck, fuck."

"You okay?" I ask, standing from my desk.

"Where is Jessica?" she asks, looking around the office.

"Oh, she had an appointment this morning. She said she'd check in after lunch."

"Oh my god, am I the only one working around here?"

I ignore the dig. She pulls out her phone, tapping furiously. "And...Milo is running late," she says, the last two words like she's making air quotes with her tone.

"Can I help with something?"

"No," she throws up her hands, but goes on, "the city is pushing back on something that should be a no-brainer, our contractor said supply costs are almost double his original estimate, and the chef that this whole thing is based around is delayed in getting to San Francisco because of some influencer trip to Miami, so I have no idea what the menu even is going to be, so no, you can't help with anything."

"Hey," I say. Her pupils are wide, her breathing rapid. Like her body thinks it's under attack.

My hand lifts instinctively—to ground her, to help. Touch always grounds me. But I stop myself. That's not what this is. Not my place.

"Take a breath," I say instead.

"Ugh, that is such a male thing to say." But she leans in a little. "Take a breath, Harper," she mocks. "You're being irrational, Harper."

"I didn't say you were being irrational," I say calmly, taking my own measured inhale. "For me, breathing nudges my nervous system out of fight or flight." I wait, watching her face. Matching my breathing to hers. "My body calms down enough that my brain can catch up."

I brace for her to scoff or turn her tirade on me. But she finally exhales the breath she was holding and pulls in a shaky inhale. I nod.

"You really think breathing fixes things?" she asks, quieter now, but she takes another inhale.

"No, not fixes things," I say, taking an involuntary step closer and exaggerating my next inhale. "It shifts blood flow back to the parts of your brain that handle decision-making instead of emergency mode, at least, it does for me."

She looks skeptical, but inhales again.

"Or, it gives you space to choose how you break."

Something unreadable crosses her face.

"I don't break," she says. Stepping back enough to slip out of my orbit and back into herself.

"Hey party people!" Milo calls from the alcove. "Happy Friday!"

"Hey, Milo," I say, grateful someone else has arrived but also disappointed that Harper and I are no longer alone. She's fun to spar with. Her control is impeccable. And I want to know what it would take to loosen it.

"I'm heading to the site," Harper says, already gathering her things, sliding her laptop into her bag with practiced efficiency. Avoidance mode engaged.

"I'll see you Monday," she says to Milo, still not looking at either of us.

She pauses in the archway, her eyes flicking back to me before settling on Milo.

"He can stay," she says quietly, then moves past him without another look.

Chapter 7

Harper

I pull the earbuds from my ears and punch in the code for the building door, still breathing hard. My thighs burn, a reminder that between work and everything else, running has slid to the bottom of my priority list.

This morning, though, I needed to burn off the restless energy buzzing under my skin after an intense week. I ran through the neighborhood, out toward Lands End, then cut back through the park—my brain drilling through every open problem like a checklist I couldn't shut down. Blake's absences. Kincade's wild demands. The ballooning costs. And we hadn't even opened yet.

My mind also wandered, annoyingly, to Max. The way he stood too close yesterday. The way my throat had tightened. And that I hated that my body responded when he told me to breathe.

That had never worked for me before.

Work more. Run faster. Push harder.

That's what works.

Not stupid breathing exercises for your stupidly hot assistant.

I linger in the lobby, dreading the single flight of stairs to my apartment, when my downstairs neighbor, Andy, bops out of her place—high ponytail swishing, gum popping, three enormous dogs straining eagerly at their leashes.

What would it be like to be that unbothered?

"Hey, Harper," she says, sliding her oversized headphones down around her neck. "You're friends with the elderly gentleman upstairs, right?"

"Yes, Mr. Evans," I say. "Walter."

"How's he doing? I haven't seen him on his daily walks as much."

"He's good," I reply automatically, but guilt pricks at me. Has he really not been getting out? I've been so buried in this Bites by Blake project that most days I've just dropped off food, or even when I stayed to watch *Wheel of Fortune* with him, I have my laptop open the whole time. I glance toward the stairs. I'll go up tonight. Get him out of the apartment.

"Well, tell him we said hello," Andy says, nodding toward the dogs now sitting obediently at her feet. "He always stops to pet the boys."

"What's this surfboard doing in the lobby?" I ask, gesturing toward the board propped against the wall as I bend to scratch behind the ears of the larger dog.

Andy's eyebrows lift. "Have you seen the owner of that surfboard?"

I look up slowly. "No."

"I bet that board's not the only thing he knows how to get wet."

A shocked laugh escapes me before I can stop it.

"What?" she chirps. "I'm just saying...I'd let him ride my wave any day."

"He shouldn't leave it here," I say, straightening. "Common areas aren't for storage."

Andy shrugs. "I don't think it's hurting anyone."

"It's in the HOA bylaws."

She pops another piece of gum into her mouth. "You don't break any rules, do you, Honeypot?"

Did she just call me Honeypot?

"Rules are there for a reason," I say.

Like my rule about not mixing work with pleasure.

"Sometimes that reason is to bend them a little." Andy shrugs. Then, in a lower voice, "Like over the back of a couch." She tips her head meaningfully toward the surfboard.

I shake my head, resolute and absolutely not thinking about couches. Or surfboards.

I pull out my phone as I start up the stairs.

Harper: *Am I an asshole?*

Amelia: *Of course not. Who said that?*

Harper: *I don't know. I just feel like sometimes I can be a little—*

I pause, thumb hovering over the screen. It's not like I'm unaware of how I come off. I have high standards. For myself, mostly. But also...everyone else.

I type: *intense.* And hit send.

Amelia: *I think you're discerning.*

Amelia: *WAIT. Is this about the kid Milo hired to be Peggy to your Draper? Did some kid call you an asshole? That asshole!*

Harper: *First of all, thank you for coming to my defense. Second, he's not a kid. He's a fully grown man.*

Amelia: *Like how "fully grown" are we talking? Old man? Or Zaddy status?*

I start to type *Zaddy* and instantly regret every life choice that led me here.

Harper: *Can I call you?*

Amelia: *Yeah—but Penelope's home, so we'll have to talk in grown-up code if you want to discuss your hot HR violation.*

I let myself into my apartment and drop onto the couch, already tapping Amelia's name.

"Auntie Harper!" Penelope shouts, and suddenly I'm staring directly into her nostril. "Guess what?"

"What, Pip?" I ask, pressing the volume down.

"My dance class is having a performance at the end of the school year."

"That sounds amazing!" I gush. "Are you practicing hard?"

Penelope averts her eyes, scrunching her nose. "We're supposed to be practicing at home."

"Ah," I say gently. "You have to put the work in when something matters to you."

She looks back at the screen and nods solemnly. "I will, Auntie Harper. I'm going to go practice right now."

"Okay, but can you put your mama on before you hang up?"

"Mom!" she yells, and I pull the phone away from my face. "Auntie Harper wants to talk to you!"

The blur of walls and floors tells me Penelope is sprinting through their house.

"Hey," Amelia says once the iPad finally steadies, propped against the backsplash while she chops vegetables for dinner. She looks tired.

"Penelope seems excited."

"She is," Amelia says, but her tone doesn't match.

"What's going on?"

"Nothing. The water heater died." She brings the knife down on a red bell pepper with more force than necessary. "I've got someone coming out, but they already said it doesn't sound fixable."

She doesn't elaborate, but I can see the numbers running behind her eyes.

"It's fine, Harper," she adds. "Don't give me that face. I'll figure it out."

I know exactly the face I'm making, the why don't you ask Penelope's deadbeat dad face, and I know better than to say it out loud.

"If you ever need help," I say, "let me know. Even if it's only a weekend getaway for you and Pip."

Her shoulders soften a fraction.

"So," Amelia pivots, wiping her hands on a dish towel. "What's the deal with this new assistant?"

I take a breath, deciding how honest to be. "Um," I exhale. "Remember the guy I told you about last weekend?"

"The one from the bar who—" She glances offscreen to make sure Penelope isn't listening, then twirls her finger vaguely in the air anyway.

"Yeah," I laugh. "Well...surprise! He's my new assistant."

"Shut the front door, Harper Wells," she shrieks, then immediately drops her voice. "You had anonymous bathroom sex with your new assistant?"

"Not sex," I whisper. "Just...you know."

A mind-blowing orgasm.

"Oh, I know," she laughs. "So, what are you two doing about it?"

"First of all, there is no 'you two,'" I say. "And second, I'm doing nothing about it."

"So, ignoring your feelings? Classic Harper move."

"I love you, but eff you. And I'm not ignoring my feelings, because there aren't any. It was a random coincidence."

"How does he feel about it?"

"I don't know. We agreed not to talk about it."

"You agreed," she says, "or you told him you weren't going to talk about it?"

"Amelia," my voice tipping into something dangerously close to a whine. "This restaurant project is going to kill me. Nothing is going according to plan, and there's so much I have to do."

"Isn't that why Milo hired someone to help?" she asks.

Exactly as I predicted, Milo's hired help is a distraction.

I just didn't expect him to have deep amber eyes and a presence that somehow calms my nerves and makes my pulse race at the same time.

Which is exactly why I need to avoid him.

"I've got to go," I say. "I need to head into the office and try to solve at least one problem."

Amelia exhales. "Maybe not everything needs to be solved today."

I end the call and grab my laptop bag. At least if I go into work on a Saturday I don't have to run into...anyone.

"Hey, surfer boy!" Andy singsongs from downstairs as I step out of my apartment onto the landing.

I can't see who she's talking to, but my first instinct is irritation. Good. I can remind the new tenant that the lobby is not a storage unit.

I start down the stairs.

And stop short.

Sullivan Maxwell Bennett is standing in the lobby of my apartment building.

My stomach drops, but heat pools low at the same time.

He's holding his surfboard under one arm, hair still damp, a soft hoodie and gray sweats slung low on his hips. He looks...comfortable. Like he belongs here.

Which is absurd.

"What are you doing here, Max?" I blurt, my voice a half-beat too fast. "Did you follow me home?"

"Ohhh," Andy coos.

"What?" Max's eyebrows shoot up as he looks between Andy and me. "No. I didn't follow you. What are you doing here?"

"I'm not telling you that," I say at the same time Andy chirps,

"She lives here, too."

"Too?" Max and I say at the same time.

"And I'm guessing," she says, eyes alight, flicking a finger between us, "you two know each other but did not know that."

She gasps theatrically. "Ohhh. Did you have a one-night stand?"

"What?" I say, mortified.

Max, infuriatingly, laughs. A real laugh, like this is the best part of his day.

"I'm very intuitive," Andy continues, nodding to herself. "You two give off strong we've touched private parts energy."

"Oh my god, Andy," I snap. My face feels hot. "Can you please give us a minute?"

"Wait," Andy holds up a finger, eyes snapping back to Max. "Didn't you say you're in town working for a restaurant consulting firm?"

Max hesitates long enough for my nerves to almost implode, then nods once.

"What a coincidence," Andy drawls, her grin turning feral. "Harper owns a restaurant consulting firm. Maybe she knows your boss."

I don't wait for either of them to respond.

"I'm leaving," I announce, heading toward the front door.

"No, no," Andy says, hands up. "Sorry. I'm sure you two have...things to discuss." She backs toward her own apartment. "I'll go inside."

"Thank you."

Andy pauses at the threshold, glancing back at Max.

"Harper wants to talk to you about rules," she says sweetly.

Then, quieter, just for me.

"Don't forget," she stage-whispers, "you can bend over for those rules too."

The door shuts behind her.

I close my eyes for exactly one second.

When I open them, Max is still there—watching me with that maddening calm, like he's already figured out what this means.

"Hey, neighbor." He smiles. "What are the chances?"

"What are the chances the universe hates me?" I ask. "Apparently very high."

He laughs, and it settles something in my chest that I don't appreciate.

"It's not that big of a deal, Harper," he says. "But I get it. You want boundaries." He shifts his weight, relaxed. "It's only a few weeks. I think we can manage to stay out of each other's way."

He pauses, then adds, lightly, "Unless you want to carpool."

"No," I say immediately.

His eyebrow lifts.

"It's like I said before," I say, folding my arms. "Do your job. Let me do mine. That's the arrangement."

"Got it," he says. "God forbid we step out of our box."

"What's that supposed to mean?"

"Just that you seem really invested in keeping everything in its proper place. Work. Home. Bar bathrooms." A small smile. "Which is fine. I get it."

My face flushes. "That's not—"

"Professional distance," he says, his eyes dimming just a bit. "I'm not looking for anything more anyway."

And I don't know why those words sting.

"Great," I say. "Neither am I."

And keep your deep breathing and your infuriatingly calm eyes to yourself.

"Alright." He tips his head toward his apartment door. His apartment mere steps from mine. "Enjoy your Saturday, Harper."

I'm about to tell him I'm heading into the office, because there is work to be done, but I don't because professional distance.

"You can't leave your surfboard in the hallway," I snap instead.

His mouth curves into an amused smile. "Noted." He disappears into his apartment.

Because rules exist for a reason.

Chapter 8

Max

"I'm heading out," Milo says, coming out of his office. He mostly works at the conference table—it's actually the first time he's been in his office since I started here. "You want to meet up for a beer later?"

"Maybe," I say, adding a few more formulas to the spreadsheet I've been working on. "I might stay in tonight, order takeout, and finish this spreadsheet."

"You're not supposed to be taking work home, Max," Milo says in his familiar big brother tone. "Remember?"

"Yeah, but this isn't really work. It's like figuring out a puzzle, it relaxes me," I justify. "Like playing *Tetris* on my phone."

"You sound like her," Milo says with affection, his chin tipping toward Harper's closed office door.

Not that I've seen her this week.

I haven't seen her since Saturday in the lobby when we discovered we live in the same building. When we agreed to professional distance.

And she's keeping her end of the bargain.

Her office door is already closed when I arrive, or she's off-site taking meetings.

I'd think she was avoiding me if I didn't know better.

This is just who she is. Workaholic. More focused on the business than the people in it. Neglecting self-care in favor of working harder.

Just like Melanie.

Hell, just like I used to be.

But I'm not that person anymore. And I won't fall back into that life.

"Harper!" Milo yells. "It's quitting time."

"Yeah," she calls back through her closed door. "I'm almost done."

"That means she'll be here for another four hours," Milo says, shaking his head with a smile. "You okay if I leave you with her?"

"You say that like she's a dangerous wild animal."

Milo shrugs.

"I'm heading out anyway," I say. "You don't have to tell me when it's quitting time. I just want to run a few more of these projections before your meeting with Blake and Kincade tomorrow."

"Oh, right," Milo says, pointing at me. "Harper said she'd take that meeting, so you can send them to her when you're done."

"Sure thing," I say. "See you tomorrow."

Milo leaves, and I double-check the last few calculations before copying the spreadsheet link into an email to hwells@studiomise.com and hit send. I shut down my laptop and gather my things when my phone buzzes.

Harper: *Your calculations are wrong.*

I scoff.

When I was six, I could recite pi to fifty-six places. When I was twelve, I won my middle school's Math Olympics. I was a computer science major before I switched to finance because my uncle told me that's where the money was.

My calculations are not wrong.

Me: *Check again. I assure you, they're not.*

Her reply comes almost immediately.

Harper: *I don't need to check again. They are.*

I stare at the message. Then at her closed office door.

She hasn't spoken five sentences to me all week, and now she's reprimanding me via text from ten feet away?

My phone buzzes again.

Harper: *But you go home. I'll fix it.*

Absolutely not.

I cross the room and knock on her door.

"Harper," I say, my voice sharper than planned.

"It's fine, Max," she calls through the door. "I'll clean this up."

"Can you open the door?" This is ridiculous. "Please?"

I hear her sigh through the wood.

"Fine. Come in."

The harsh overhead lights are off when I enter, replaced by the glow of half a dozen lamps scattered around her office. The space feels warmer than I expected. Softer. Less like the command center I've built in my head and more like somewhere someone actually enjoys spending time.

Harper sits behind her desk, the late-evening sun slanting through the window at her back, catching in her dark hair. Her lipstick is still vivid red, like she reapplied it recently. My gaze snags on the clean line of her collarbone visible at the wide neck of her gray sweater.

The same collarbone I kissed just over a week ago.

I shut down that thought.

"My calculations aren't wrong," I say, resting my hands on the back of the chair opposite her desk. "I double-checked everything."

She doesn't answer right away. Her eyes flick—just once—to my forearms flexing when my fingers curl around the chair. I straighten, stepping back.

"I'm confident they're accurate," I add. Less defensive. More factual.

Harper swallows, turning back to her screen, fingers tapping as she pulls something up. Her brow furrows as she studies the numbers.

"It doesn't make sense," she says, more to herself than to me. She taps a few keys, then flips through the printed pages spread across her desk. "If your calculations are right, why are they so different from Kincade's projections?"

I step closer without meaning to.

"Are you admitting my numbers are right?"

She snorts softly—almost a smile. "Your math might be right," she concedes. "But these numbers are still off."

I circle behind her desk and pick up the pages she's been studying. "They're only off if we're modeling the same assumptions," I say, scanning the columns. "Which I don't think we are."

I don't look up from the papers, but I can feel her eyes on me like a weight.

"What are these tracking to?" I ask, pointing to a block of figures.

"RevPASH," she says like I should already know.

"The...rev what?"

"Revenue per available seat hour." She's already reaching for a pencil from the gold cup on her desk. She flips a page over and starts writing. "Seats times average check times table turns." She scratches numbers on the page and does the math—accurately and quickly—in her head. "Alcohol can drastically increase the average check but also the dwell time."

She adds another figure, then looks back at the screen.

I move closer, placing my hand on the back of her chair. Close enough to see the formulas on her screen. Close enough to catch her perfume—warm, subtle, and annoyingly familiar.

"You're modeling steady operations," I say. "He's projecting hype."

She stills.

"But hype can't be systematized," I add.

"Exactly."

"This Blake guy...he's a TikTok sensation, right?"

She spins her chair toward me, peering up through dark lashes. "Yeah. Why?"

I lean my hip against the edge of her desk, bringing myself closer to her eye line. This is the first time we've really been in the same room all week.

"So his followers are going to be the primary customer base?"

"That's the hope," she says.

"Do they take photos of their food?"

She leans in, and a wide smile spreads across her lips. Finally.

"Probably," she chuckles.

"I hate when people do that," I say, my gaze locked on hers now.

"Something we agree on," she says, her voice dropping a little lower. She uncrosses and recrosses her legs toward me.

"That adds time per table," I say. "Slows the whole night down."

"Fuck, you're right."

She shoves her chair back and presses her fingers to her temple, eyes closing. Not in defeat. I can practically see the gears turning.

She's plotting.

I recognize that look—the mix of stubborn determination and raw brainpower it takes to crack something that refuses to cooperate.

When she opens her eyes, there's a distant focus to them, like she's already halfway somewhere else. She stands, leans back over the desk, and starts scribbling numbers on the back of Kincade's proposal, muttering to herself as if I'm not even in the room.

It's mesmerizing.

I step back, giving her space, watching her work. The flex of muscle in her arms as she grips the pencil. The way her brow furrows, then smooths. The slight sway of her hips as she leans forward, completely absorbed.

I shove my hand into my pocket to keep from reaching for her.

Then, without warning, she straightens and strides out of the office.

I'm left standing, staring at the doorway, wondering what the hell just happened.

A moment later, she's back with arms full of the architectural plans Milo left spread across the conference table. She didn't bother rolling them up first, just dumps them onto her desk and spreads them out over everything else, unapologetic chaos.

"What if we..." She grabs a piece of discarded paper and lays it over the blueprints. I can see the sketches taking shape.

"Yeah." I nod, picking up the calculations she did earlier, looking between the numbers and the markings she's adding to the restaurant's layout. "Hand me that pencil."

She hands it over her shoulder, and I swear, there are sparks where our fingers brush when I take it. But she pulls away as quickly, back to her additions.

"If we move this..." She's drawing long slashes across the blueprint, then turns to look back at me. "Can you—"

"Already did," I say, sinking down in her desk chair and adding new calculations to the numbers she'd plotted earlier.

She shifts her body, leaning to reach the far side of the desk, a move that practically drapes her over my lap. Her sweater rides up, exposing a sliver of skin at her waist, and my dick responds involuntarily.

Fuck.

"Did that work?" she asks, turning her head to look back over her shoulder at me. Her cheeks are flushed, and her breathing is labored. And I'm not thinking of restaurant calculations.

"Uh..." I stammer, pushing the chair back and standing. I tear my eyes away from the dip of her low back and the curve of her ass bent over her desk and force myself to look at the numbers. I take the pencil again and finish the calculation, my pulse ticking up as the final number settles into place.

"Perfect."

Harper stands quickly, spinning to face me. I'm closer than she realized. Close enough that she bumps into my chest.

My hands come up instinctively to steady her, one resting on the slope of her waist, the other on the curve of her bicep. I should let go.

I don't.

"It works?" Her eyes are bright, breathless.

"It works," I say.

Her hand lands on my chest, not pushing away, just...there. I'm sure she can feel my heart hammering through her palm.

"We did it?" she asks, but her smile tells me she already knows.

"We did it," I confirm.

We're standing too close. I know it. She knows it.

But neither of us move.

I wait for her to push me away. Create distance. Retreat behind her walls.

But she doesn't.

Her eyes drop to my mouth, then back up.

My hand slides from her arm to the back of her neck, fingers threading into the short hairs at her nape.

Her lips part on an exhale.

Our mouths are so close we are breathing the same air. She fists her hand in my shirt, tugging me toward her.

"Harper!" Milo's voice booms from the front door, and we both jump apart. "I could see the lights in your office still on—oh!" he says, surprised as he walks in. Harper is back at her desk, leaning over the drawings. I'm pacing with the calculations, a respectable five feet away. "Max, I didn't realize you were still here."

"He was just..." Harper stands, smoothing her sweater down.

"Harper caught a mistake I'd made in the calculations, not fully understanding industry norms," I say.

"Max helped me think outside the box to address a dwell issue," Harper adds, gesturing to the schematic on her desk. Milo rounds the corner and peers down.

"Oh, this is good." He keeps talking, but I'm barely listening.

All I can think about is how close Harper's mouth was to mine. How easily she fit against me.

And I'm suddenly very aware of how close I came to crossing a line I swore I wouldn't cross again.

"I'll leave you to it," Milo finishes, clearly addressing something I wasn't paying attention to.

"I should head out," I say, purposefully walking toward the door. "See you both tomorrow."

"Max," Harper says, stopping me in my tracks.

I turn back, careful to keep my expression neutral.

She watches me for a beat, long enough that something unguarded flickers across her face. Longing? Regret? Maybe both.

"Goodnight," she says, already turning back to her computer.

"Night," I say.

I turn toward the door, but something makes me glance back. Her eyes are closed, one finger grazing her bottom lip.

My hand tightens on the doorframe. Every instinct screams to go back. To cross the room. The line. To finish what we started.

Instead, I leave before she opens her eyes.

Chapter 9

Harper

I've been avoiding Max for three days.

Three days since we almost kissed in my office. Three days since I felt his fingers threading through my hair. Three days since Milo walked in and I remembered why this is a terrible idea.

Professional distance. That's what we agreed to.

Since that night, I've timed my arrivals to miss him. Taken meetings off-site. Emailed instead of walking ten feet to his desk.

He's done the same. Early surf sessions that keep him out until I'm at my desk. Mumbled apologies to Milo about traffic. Eyes that won't quite meet mine.

It should feel like relief.

Instead, it feels like the air before a thunderstorm—thick, electric, ready to break.

And now we're standing in the ground-floor lobby of the financial district high-rise that houses Kincade's offices because Milo got stuck in another meeting and it's now only the two of us presenting.

Just me and Max.

Alone.

I've been trying not to stare at his forearms for the past ten minutes while he reviews the presentation on his phone.

The way his sleeves are rolled up. The flex of muscle when he scrolls. The view in those khakis doing unexplainable things to my focus.

The tension is unbearable.

"I think we need to get this out of our system," I say before my brain has fully caught up with my mouth.

Max looks up from his phone. "Get what out of our system?"

This is a serious meeting. I need to focus.

"This." I gesture vaguely between us. "It's like Skittles."

"I'm not sure I follow."

"I had a Skittles phase in high school," I say. "I was eating them every day. So, I bought a pound bag and ate the entire thing while watching the season finale of *The O.C.*"

Max's mouth tilts. "The entire bag?"

"Yes." I don't mention puking all over the bathroom later that night. "And it worked. Haven't wanted them since."

He studies me for a beat. "Am I the Skittles in this analogy?"

"Yes. I mean—no." I exhale. "There's clearly...something unresolved between us."

His brow lifts, but he doesn't interrupt.

"And it's distracting," I finish. "For both of us."

"This is the slowest elevator in history," he mutters, jabbing the call button again.

The doors finally slide open, and Max holds them as I step inside. A man in a badly tailored suit rushes in after me.

"So," Max says, leaning closer, "you're saying the only way to get over a craving is to give in completely?"

"Shh," I whisper. "But yes."

The elevator lurches upward, stopping two floors later. Three women pile in, chatting loudly. I edge closer to Max as the space tightens, my shoulder brushing his arm.

"When we pass twelve," I continue quietly, "no one else gets on or off. We'll have it to ourselves until the top."

He swallows. The way his throat moves does something to my insides I don't have time to examine. I need to eat the entire bag of Skittles if I'm going to get any work done over the next three months.

"We'll have eighteen floors," I add, barely audible now, "to get this out of our system."

He scoffs, still not looking at me—like he's trying very hard no to. Like maybe he's going to tell me to go to hell. The doors open on nine. Two more people cram in, forcing him closer. His hand lands lightly at the base of my spine.

On ten, a woman with a massive tote squeezes in, and Max shifts instinctively, turning his body to shield me from the press. His mouth is suddenly right by my ear.

"So once we're alone," his breath is warm against my skin, "what do you want me to do?"

Electricity zips straight down my spine. I close my eyes for half a second, steadying myself.

"You'll figure it out," I say on a quiet exhale.

Most of the elevator empties on eleven. Max steps back, but his hand doesn't leave my waist. Instead, it shifts, slipping beneath the hem of my blazer, brushing the silk of my blouse—a whisper of heat and pressure.

The trip up a single floor feels endless. I can hear his breathing, feel the tension coiled in his body. The quiet hum of the elevator is the only sound between us.

Finally, the doors slide open. The woman exits, glancing back once. Max nods politely as the doors close again.

I assume I'll have to make the first move.

I don't.

The second the elevator lurches into motion, Max backs me into the wall, one hand firm at my waist, the other lifting my chin so my eyes meet his. He pauses—just a breath—searching my face.

I nod once.

His mouth claims mine, the kiss urgent and unhurried at the same time. His fingers dig into my hip as he steps closer, slotting his thigh between my legs. I open for him without thinking.

He groans softly when I nip at his lower lip, the sound vibrating against my mouth and sliding down my throat, settling in my core.

I grab his ass and pull him closer, desperate for friction. For more.

“Harper,” he breathes. His hand slips between my jacket, cupping my breast, possessive enough to steal my breath. He stills, just for a second.

“Yes,” I gasp, kissing him harder, needier now.

My gaze flicks up to the glowing numbers above the doors. 15. 16. 17.

I slam my palm against the emergency button.

The elevator jolts to a stop.

“How long?” Max starts, breathless, his mouth already moving down the column of my throat.

“Just...” I try to say, don’t stop, but Max reads my mind, my desire—or maybe his. He claims my mouth again, his kisses shifting from exploratory to desperate. I reach between us and palm him through his dress pants. He’s hard, and a sound slips from me, somewhere between a groan and a whimper. For one wild second, I want to drop to my knees.

“Fuck,” he swears, his head tipping back as I squeeze harder, my hand already moving toward his belt buckle. He sucks in a sharp breath and circles my wrist gently, stilling me.

My breathing is ragged, fractured. His eyes—those deep amber pools—make me want to do something reckless. Dangerous. I try to reach for him again, but his other hand cups my jaw, soft but firm enough to hold our lips apart.

His thumb brushes across my cheek, and he presses a chaste kiss to my undeniably swollen lips. His hand lingers at my waist long enough for me to feel the choice he's making, before he lets go. Then he straightens the lapels of my jacket and turns so we're standing shoulder to shoulder once more.

Got it. We're done.

That was all he wanted. Or all he was willing to give.

I run my fingers through my hair. Tuck my blouse back in where it had escaped and stare straight ahead, unable to look at him.

He reaches out and disengages the emergency stop.

The elevator begins its ascent again. And the rejection stings more than it should.

I was supposed to be in control of this. Get him out of my system and move on.

Instead, he stopped me.

And fuck if I'm not craving Skittles.

Chapter 10

Max

"Wells!"

A man in dark jeans and a black shirt—unbuttoned one too many for a professional setting—strides toward Harper with his arms outstretched. Harper lets him hug her, but her body language is stiff, already looking past him. The sharp twist in my gut loosens.

"Kincade," she says, stepping back and gesturing to me. "This is Max Bennett. He's helping me on this project."

"Helping?" he laughs. "Since when do you let anyone help you?"

"I'm getting coffee and keeping files organized," I say, extending my hand. A little self-deprecation disarms men like Kincade.

He takes my hand—but he's still talking to Harper. "Because if you do need help, I'd be happy to spend more time with you."

I tighten my grip until it forces his attention back to me. "Nice to meet you, Kincade," I say. "That won't be necessary."

He narrows his eyes, sizing me up.

"Can we run through the projections?" Harper says, already turning toward Kincade's office. "Is Blake running late?"

"Yeah, he should be here soon," Kincade says, following her. "Said he has menu concepts to run past you."

I pull out Harper's chair. She doesn't look at me when she sits.

Her hair is slightly mussed. A corner of her blouse is still untucked. I take the seat beside her, uncomfortably aware of how close we still feel. Of how unresolved this still is.

She made it very clear this was just a craving she wanted to get out of her system.

And I should be able to do that. Kiss a beautiful woman in an elevator and walk away. Keep it casual. Keep it simple.

But I know myself. If I let myself start, I'd never be able to quit her.

I'll want more. And she's already told me there isn't any.

So I stopped. Before I go too deep.

Even if stopping nearly killed me.

"These projections are looking great, Harps," Kincade says.

I glance at Harper. She's annoyed.

So am I.

"I love what you did, shifting the bar area for a dedicated Instagram station," he continues. "Really smart."

Harper catches my eye for a beat, barely a smile, before turning back to Kincade.

"By giving patrons different areas, we increase dwell time without decreasing RevPASH," Harper says. "And creative, photographable cocktails will keep people there while tables turn."

"Harper," Kincade shakes his head. "I don't know how you do it all."

Her eyes flick to mine again, a slight blush on her cheeks.

Kincade's phone buzzes. "Blake's here," he says, standing. "Meeting us in the East Conference room with some," he does air quotes, "bites to try."

Kincade leads us down the hall into a conference room. At the head of the table, a young man—a kid really—stands up, rubbing his hands together.

"Harper," Kincade bellows, holding his arms wide. "This is our golden goose, Blake Adams."

He can't be more than twenty. Jeans and a backwards baseball hat.

"Hey, Ms. Wells," he says, holding out his hand. "It's nice to finally meet you."

"Harper's fine," Harper says. I catch her assessing eye dropping over him. Her brain calculating the image upgrade he's going to need.

"Max," I say, holding out my hand, mostly to pull Harper's intense stare from the poor kid.

"Okay, so I'm a little nervous," Blake says, turning to the trays topped with silver food domes behind him. "But I prepared my three most viral dishes for you to try."

"These are the items everyone will be coming in for," Kincade interjects, beating me to pulling out Harper's chair. She doesn't let on, just sits and scoots in herself.

"This one got over three million views," Blake says, placing a plate of rice in front of Harper.

She scoops rice and toppings onto her fork and takes a bite. She chews with what looks like...determination, before smiling, a little forced, nodding. But she doesn't speak. She continues to nod for an unnaturally long time before covering her mouth with a closed fist and swallowing.

"Interesting," she says, her voice tipping up at the end, almost like a question.

"Yeah?" Blake asks hopefully. "Okay, great, yeah, great," he stammers, pulling a second plate off the tray.

Harper slides the first away, but when I go to pick up my fork, she places her fingers on my thigh, still smiling up at Blake. A silent warning.

"Okay, so this second one is a little different, but it got over two million likes."

"And it hasn't even been up for a month," Kincade adds. "Those numbers are going to grow."

Blake isn't telling us anything about the dish. I peer over the plate. Some sort of meat, but I can't tell what.

"He shot this one from a different angle," Kincade says, scrolling his phone. "His community loved it."

I glance at Harper, and she looks scared. I pick up my fork and hover it over the plate. "May I?" I ask quietly.

She nods and leans back.

"Holy shit!" I exclaim as soon as the food hits my tongue. Harper's eyes snap to mine—wide.

"Right?" Kincade slaps my back as I reach for my water glass, taking a long sip. "That's what I said when I tried it too. People aren't going to see that coming."

It was spicy—really spicy—but I grew up in Jackson Heights, so I could handle heat. My childhood best friend's nani used to serve us a goat curry that made your eyes water, and you'd still ask for seconds.

What Blake served was just bad.

Harper watches me with concern and a silent plea. I shake my head once, almost imperceptibly, and push the dish forward.

"We are on a roll now." Kincade claps his hands together. "Blake, you are going to kill the shit out of this restaurant."

"Kill something," I whisper to Harper. She lets out a little laugh, and something like pride swells in my chest.

"Last," Blake says, placing a slice of chocolate cake in front of Harper. "This is the first dish that went viral."

Harper stares at the cake, turning the plate like she's assessing damage. She takes a fortifying inhale and takes a bite. And bursts into laughter, placing her hand on her chest. Then she pushes the plate toward me.

I take a bite.

"You'll never guess what it is," Kincade says, beaming.

"Um..." I swallow, thinking planting soil and sugar can't be right.

"Mushrooms," Blake answers.

"And you can pick your level of psychotropic!" Kincade puts his hands up in a touchdown gesture.

"What?" I say, as Harper reaches for her napkin to spit out her cake.

"Don't worry!" Blake assures. "This is the virgin chocolate cake. I wouldn't do that without your consent," he says solemnly.

Twenty minutes later, Harper and I say our goodbyes. She promises to "circle back" on the menu concepts once she's had time to run some numbers, and we step out into the cool San Francisco air.

"What. The. Fuck," Harper says.

Then she bursts into laughter, burying her face in her hands.

"I'm not even sure what to say," I offer. "Psychedelic mushroom chocolate cake?"

She laughs harder as we walk toward the corner, and without thinking, my hand settles at the small of her back, steering us away from the building.

"That rice dish was basically uncooked and bland," she says, glancing up at me.

"And I think I lost at least three layers of skin off my tongue from whatever that mystery meat was," I add. "And I grew up on Mrs. Patel's vindaloo."

Harper shakes her head, still smiling, and for a second—despite how awful that food was—it feels...nice. Like we've unlocked some shared disaster we can laugh about later. An inside joke that belongs only to us.

"Well," I say, "at least we have a story for our grandkids—"

Fuck.

"I mean. Our individual grandkids."

She snorts. “The time we tried to open a restaurant with a chef who couldn’t cook?”

We stop at the corner.

Her smile fades.

“Max,” she says, her voice small. “I’m so fucked.”

She exhales, running a hand through her hair.

“We can’t open a restaurant if the chef can’t cook,” she says, face buried in her hands.

“Hey,” I say, trying to catch her eye. “Do you want to go somewhere and brainstorm? I bet we can come up with a solution together.”

She’s already pulling out her phone, thumbs flying across the screen. She barely looks up.

“No,” Harper says, distracted. “I need to go back to the office.”

“Sure. Let’s go.”

“No, I—” She looks up then, really looks at me, just for a second. Something flickers in her expression before she shakes her head and drops her gaze back to her phone. “I need to go alone.”

“Of course you do.” It comes out sharper than I expected.

“What does that mean?”

“I get that you don’t want anything...more.” I shove my hand through my hair. “We are both clear on that. But we can solve problems together. We’re good together. Let me help you.”

“I don’t need your help,” she says, but her voice wavers slightly.

“Of course you don’t, that’s the problem.”

She stares at me, and something flashes in her eyes. Hurt. Anger. Maybe both.

“You don’t know anything about me,” she says quietly.

“You’re right,” I say. “I don’t. Because you won’t let me.”

She looks away. “I have to go.”

Her Waymo approaches the curb. She doesn't look back, but I notice a slight falter as she climbs in. The way her shoulders are hunched, the death grip on her phone.

Something in my chest tightens—not with anger, but recognition.

I was Harper.

Three years ago, skipping meals and calling it dedication. Waking up at 3 a.m. drenched in sweat. Migraines so bad I'd throw up in the trash can under my desk while my Zoom call was on mute. Insisting I was fine. That I didn't need any help. That I could handle it.

Until I couldn't.

I pull out my phone, then put it back.

What would I even say? "Hey, I know I just yelled at you, but I'm worried you're going to have a breakdown in a parking lot like I did."

She wouldn't listen.

I wouldn't have either.

You can't save someone who doesn't think they're drowning.

Chapter 11
Harper

I start up the stairs, takeout in one hand, my heels in the other. The building is quiet—late, but not that late. I wasn't at the office for hours. I couldn't focus.

I barely made it past the meltdown I had over the shitshow that is our star restaurant project. The one that's supposed to put Studio Mise on the map. The one I need to prove I can do this my way—without the patriarchal bullshit.

So I stomped my feet. Literally. Screamed into my throw pillows—my preferred coping mechanism—then ordered takeout, intending to stay as late as it took to fix everything. But that familiar pressure behind my right eye, a warning I've been ignoring for hours, made it hard to look at a screen.

I thought about calling Milo. But I didn't need to bother him. I could figure this out on my own.

By the time my pho arrived—from the place on Castro, obviously—my eyes were so blurry from tears I didn't even remember crying that I couldn't see.

So I left.

I thought about stopping at Bar None. Seeing if whiskey could solve my problem. But I knew I just needed my bed.

I glance over my shoulder at the mailboxes in the lobby. My eyes snag on apartment 1A.

I should check my mail, I think, crossing back toward the boxes.

I pause at Max's door.

He's probably asleep. Didn't he tell me that first night he used to be a night owl, but never stays up late anymore?

God, that night at Bar None. Or yesterday in the elevator. My insides pull tight at the memory, at realizing I wanted more. I lean my ear close to the door, hearing faint music, jazz maybe, from inside.

I glance down at the bag of too much food I ordered. Then knock quietly.

No response.

He's probably asleep. I turn and head back up the stairs.

"Harper?" Max calls when I'm almost to the first landing.

"Oh, hey," I say, unsure why I knocked, but I take a few steps back down. Max leans in his open doorway.

He's barefoot, in low-slung gray sweatpants resting on the jut of his hipbone, a black tank pulled tight across his chest.

His eyes scan over me, not appreciative, assessing. Like he's checking for damage.

I shift my weight, suddenly self-conscious.

"I ordered too much food," I say by way of explanation.

Max nods but doesn't reply. He's not going to let me off the hook that easily. And I actually respect him for that. I was an asshole, and that was not an apology.

"Look, I'm sorry about earlier. I know you were trying to help. I just get a little..."

"Singularly focused when it comes to work?" Max finishes, his voice a little flat.

"Yeah, something like that." I shift again. "But the Blake disaster. The RevPASH thing. We do work well together. As coworkers."

His expression shifts for half a second, then smooths.

"You've been a big help around the office and...to me," I continue. "Thank you."

Max's gaze flicks from the food in one hand to my heels in the other. He pulls his lower lip between his teeth and looks up at the ceiling, like he's gathering his strength. Or his willpower.

"Do you want to come in?" he says, but it's a little forced.

"I don't want to..." I swallow, "put you out. It's late."

He looks at me for a long second, like he's weighing something.

"Come in, Harper." It lands like a command, not an invitation.

I follow Max inside and take in his apartment. I've been inside this unit before, back when the landlord was showing it—same short-term rental setup, the same boring gray furniture and dark wood finishes. But Max has managed to make it feel lived-in. Intentional.

The overhead lights are off, replaced by the warm glow of lamps. My preferred vibe. The jazz I heard earlier is coming from an impressive stereo setup, anchored by a vintage-looking record player. A stack of books sits on the coffee table, a cozy blanket draped over the arm of the sofa.

It feels like him. Calm. Grounded. Thoughtful.

Max takes the food from my hand and moves through the kitchen, pulling bowls from a cabinet. The motion lifts his shirt just enough to expose the hard curve of his obliques, his shoulder flexing as he reaches.

I've never actually seen him naked.

That feels unfair now.

"Is this the infamous pho Milo's been raving about?" Max asks, setting the bowls down and pulling me out of my daydream.

"It is," I say, hoping he doesn't catch the slight strain in my voice.

He ladles the soup into two bowls and grabs a pair of deep ceramic spoons—clearly not part of the apartment's standard-issue inventory.

"Beer?"

"Sure," I say, grateful for something uncomplicated to agree to.

We settle at the two-person table in front of the window that overlooks the street. The same view from my apartment upstairs. Everything is a little sharper here. With the glow of the streetlight, I can make out the garden wall where I saw Andy setting up some sort of fairy house the other day. Penelope would love it. I have to remember to show it to her if I can convince Amelia to visit.

Max pops the cap on one of the beer bottles, handing it across the table to me, before popping his own. He holds out the neck of the bottle, and I clink mine against it.

"What are we toasting?" I ask, taking a sip.

"I'm not sure yet." He's watching me, his gaze intense enough that I have to look away. "Did you figure out how to teach Blake to cook by the soft open?"

I huff out a laugh and shake my head, then gesture to the takeout soup. "You're pretty much looking at the extent of my cooking these days."

I look at the label. It's good, from a small-batch brewery in Berkeley. "We did a collab with them and a food truck as one of Studio Mise's first projects."

"When was that?"

"Almost two years ago."

Max slurps a spoonful of the pho's broth, clearly not his first time eating Vietnamese food. "Oh, this is good."

"Told you," I smile. "But you must get good Vietnamese in New York."

"I've lived on both coasts, here's my take," Max says, reclining back in his chair. My eyes dip to his shoulder flexing as he drapes it over the back of his chair. "Nothing in Manhattan can beat a Mission taqueria. But if you want a solid pastrami on rye, SF has attempts, but NYC has institutions."

I laugh and lean closer, folding my arms on the table. "So, you do know something about the restaurant industry."

He copies me, pushing his bowl forward to rest one elbow on the table. "Like I said, mostly just eating at them."

I let my eyes travel from his eyes—those pools I can never tear away from—down the high arch of his cheekbone, the sharp angle of his jaw. There's something hard and soft about everything with Max. The defined muscle of his arms, but the gentle way he moves. The sharp intelligence in his eyes, but the warmth when he smiles. The careful distance he keeps, but the way his body leans toward mine anyway.

He's watching me watch him.

And he doesn't look away.

"California wins the whole farm-to-table vibe," Max continues, pulling my focus back. "But you can eat anything you want at 2 a.m. in New York, and that's not the case here."

"I thought you weren't a night owl. How do you know what's available at 2 a.m.?"

"Harper," he says my name like I want him to say it again. "I was a night owl and an early bird. For many, many years."

"Finance, right?"

He nods and returns to his soup bowl. I trace the line of his neck down to where his collarbone disappears beneath his tank top. The same collarbone I kissed at Bar None. The same chest I pressed against in the elevator.

My fingers itch to touch him. But that's not what this is.

"Why did you leave?" I ask. "New York, I mean. Or finance, or—" I stop when I notice he's stopped eating, his eyes fixed on his bowl of noodles "—nevermind, I didn't mean to overstep." I spoon a large scoop of my soup into my mouth to replace my foot.

"I left finance," he starts carefully, glancing up at me through dark lashes, "because I was having panic attacks that led to a mental health breakdown."

"Oh."

"I left New York because my marriage couldn't handle the fallout," he says, "and because Milo offered me a job."

"Max, I'm sorry, I shouldn't have..."

"It's okay. It was almost eighteen months ago," he says, his voice returning to its normal deep tone. "Luckily, I had enough savings to step back and regroup. And my therapist says it's good for me to talk about it...with people I trust."

"You trust me?" I say, somewhat surprised.

"Yeah," he laughs. "I do, maybe despite my best interests."

"You can talk more about it," I say softly. "If you want."

"Things were hard for a while," he says.

"But you're better now?"

"I'm not sure if it's something you get better from," he replies honestly. "But I've learned how to manage it. The way my brain works."

"Like the meditation?" I ask, thinking about the morning I walked in on him.

"Yeah, and therapy and medication if I need it," he says honestly. "And surfing."

"Right," I say.

"I promise," he holds up his hands, "never to leave my surfboard in the hallway again."

"God, I am a crotchety old neighbor, aren't I?" I say, thinking of the time I yelled at Cal's sister and friend for making out on the landing.

"No, you have high standards," he says. "You like things done a certain way. And you'll go to the mat for something—or someone—once you believe in it. You're an Enneagram Eight."

I narrow my eyes. "Have you been talking to Milo?"

Max laughs, a big, genuine boom that sends a warm feeling into my chest, settling behind my ribs.

"You should come with me one morning," he says. His wide smile replaced with something serious.

"Surfing? I don't know how."

"Good thing I can teach you. It's a great way to start your day. It clears your mind."

"I think my mind would worry about sharks the whole time." But now I'm picturing Max in one of those surfing ads, his wetsuit pulled down, exposing his chest.

"Nah, they don't bother you," Max says with a smirk. "And I can't tell you the number of problems I've solved bobbing in the water at sunrise. Maybe it would give you some clarity around Blake."

"Sunrise surfing feels...aspirational," I say. "I don't really do mornings that involve joy."

"Well, the offer stands," he says, and it feels like just that. An offer. Not a must-do, or a challenge, or a test.

The quiet stretches between us, thick and dangerous. The kind that invites bad decisions. Or honest ones. I'm not sure which scares me more.

I glance at the empty bowls on the table, at his bare feet on the hardwood, at the way his attention is fully on me without asking for anything in return. It would be so easy to make my usual choice here. Take what I want and figure the rest out later.

Not this time. We're coworkers. And neighbors. I need to leave it at that.

I stand, reaching for my heels. "I should go."

His brow furrows slightly. "You sure?"

That's the problem. I'm not.

"Yeah. I should."

He walks me to the door, leaning against the doorframe like he did when I first arrived.

"Thanks for the food," he says. "And...for coming by."

For a second, I think about kissing him goodnight. But that's not what this is.

"Thanks for not leaving your surfboard in the hallway anymore," I joke, and Max chuckles.

"See you tomorrow, Harper," he says, stepping back, resting his hand on the doorknob.

My pulse is thrumming. I should say something that will keep him from shutting the door. My body feels awake in a way it hasn't in a long time—wanting, yes, but also something else. Something heavier. Stickier.

Be smart, I tell myself. Be disciplined.

"Tomorrow then," I say, forcing a smile.

I take a step back, and Max nods once, his eyes closing for a beat. Then he returns my smile and shuts the door.

Chapter 12

Max

I pour coffee into my favorite mug, still half asleep, and nearly miss it entirely.

It was well past midnight when Harper left last night. And I spent at least another hour awake, staring at the ceiling, replaying the evening—every laugh, every pause, every moment I chose restraint over instinct.

Including the infuriating decision not to ask her to stay.

It had felt like the right call. Necessary. We agreed to be coworkers, to work together. Keep it simple. Keep professional distance. That's what I thought I wanted. I came here to do a job. And do it well.

But I'd be lying to myself if I said that felt like enough.

Everything between Harper and me started transactional. A coping mechanism for stress. A dive-bar hookup. An elevator make-out. Two people agreeing to get something out of their system.

I snort quietly into my coffee.

Like I could ever get her out of my system.

I thought Harper was the kind of woman I didn't want anymore. The must succeed at all costs. The work before everything. Using sex to distract from stress. But watching her walk away from me yesterday, I saw the cracks. The strain she wasn't letting anyone see. This whole time I've compared her to Melanie. But she's not, she's me.

Melanie worked for ego. Harper works because she cares too much.

The way she shows up for Milo, not just as a business partner, but as a friend who knows when to push and when to back off. The way her voice softens when she talks to her best friend's daughter on the phone, patient and encouraging in a way she never is with herself. The way she checked on me yesterday when the spicy food hit, concern flickering across her face before she could hide it behind a joke.

She cares. Deeply. But she doesn't let herself show it.

Until a conversation that started about the best burrito spot in SF and ended with me sharing things I don't normally share outside of my therapist's couch changed that. Harper didn't flinch. She didn't make me feel shame, like Melanie had, or try to fix me like my family had. She just...listened.

She lives by compartments. Clear lines. Distinct buckets. Sex over here. Friendship over there. Work towering above it all. Or so I thought.

I don't want only one piece of her.

I rub a hand over my face and lean against the counter. What the hell am I doing?

Fuck if I couldn't picture the whole goddamned thing when I opened the door to find her there, heels in one hand, takeout in the other. I forced us to sit at the table, a safe square of distance between us, because what I really wanted was to pull her onto the couch, haul her feet into my lap, and rub away the tension while we strategized together.

Fuck.

It was a good thing I dragged myself out of bed this morning to go surfing. I needed the clarity I'd promised Harper the ocean and the salt air could provide.

I drain the rest of my coffee and retrieve my board from my bedroom.

Saltwater cures all.

At least I hope.

I pull open my door—

—and stop short.

Harper stands in the hallway in oversized sweats, a puffy jacket, and an Iron Cats baseball cap pulled low over her eyes, the tips of her dark bob peeking out beneath it.

"Hey," I say.

She looks up. "You promise I won't get eaten by a shark?"

I nod, warmth blooming in my chest before I can stop it. "Yeah. I promise. Hang on," I say, turning back into the apartment. "I have a wetsuit you can wear."

"God, it's beautiful out here," she says. We're both straddling our boards, bobbing in the calm water.

She's right. It's a perfect morning.

It's actually a shitty morning for surfing. There's no surf to speak of. But that made it easy to show Harper the basics near shore and to paddle out farther. When she wanted to "catch a wave," I told her most of surfing isn't actually surfing.

She scoffed. "How do you know I'm not good at patience?"

"Because I never was either."

So we'd paddled out past where the swells would break and just floated. The other regulars had figured out there were no waves today, so we had Ocean Beach practically to ourselves.

"You do this every morning?" Harper asks, angling toward me.

"I try." I paddle closer, not wanting us to drift too far apart.

At least that's what I tell myself.

"When Milo suggested I move out here, I made a deal with myself to surf as much as I could before I go back to New York."

Harper's head snaps toward me, something unreadable flashing across her face before she turns back to the horizon. "Not too much surfing in New York, I guess."

"During hurricane season, you can," I say. "Not like here, though. I picked the apartment complex because of its proximity to the beach."

"So did I," she agrees. "But more for the checkbox of 'own property near the beach.'" She looks out over the rising sun, casting everything in gold. "I thought I would come down here more when I bought the place. But I never do. Too busy, I guess."

I watch her face. The way it falls. The long breath she takes.

I get it. Just one more milestone, one more success, then I can enjoy what I've worked for. But the goalposts keep moving. Or we keep moving them on ourselves.

"There's a great little fish and chips restaurant over there called Mama's," I say, hitching my thumb back toward the avenues. I don't suggest we go sometime.

She laughs, "I think you know more about the SF restaurant scene than I do."

"I like to eat." I shrug.

The sun is fully up now. Later than I usually stay out here. Much later than Harper usually gets to the office.

"We should probably head in," I say.

Harper sighs, "Yeah, I guess."

I smile despite myself. "Did I convert you?"

"I think I understand what you mean. Something out here makes you clearer on what you need."

Her words land in my chest like a victory. Like she accepted my invitation to my secret world.

"Or what you want," she adds. Those words make my dick respond.

I lie down on my board, hiding my erection, and she follows as we paddle toward shore. It's too much work to talk while we fight the current, and that's probably a good thing, because I want to ask what she means. What she wants. Probably a solution to the Blake thing. That's why we came out here.

We reach shore, both breathing hard. The morning air is cold. She shivers and wraps her arms around herself. I gesture up the beach. "There are showers up there. You can warm up and get the salt off."

"Yeah, good idea."

We trudge up the beach in silence. Her last words hang between us. We pause at the cement building. She points at the "women" sign. "I'll be quick."

"Take your time."

Ten minutes pass, then fifteen. She really does take her time. I'd peeled off my wetsuit, rinsed off, and pulled on my sweats, thinking she'd be in a hurry to get home and into the office. But at the twenty-minute mark, I lean into the doorway. The water's still running.

"Harper?" I call.

"Max!" she gasps out, and everything inside me tightens with panic.

"What's wrong?" I call, taking a step in.

"I'm...shit...stuck."

"What do you mean?"

"I can't get out of my wetsuit. Can you..." thrashing sounds. "Can you help me?"

Harper Wells just asked for help.

"Of course," I say, pausing. "Is there anyone else in there?"

"If there were someone else in here, I wouldn't still be stuck, would I?" she shouts. I smile despite myself.

I round the cement wall and find Harper standing in the stream of water. Her cheeks are flushed, and she's shivering, breathing like she's sprinted from a tiger.

"I can't. Reach. The. Zipper," she grunts out, trying to grab the frayed end of the zipper pull.

"Here," I rush toward her, not caring that my pants are getting wet. She turns her back, and I guide the zipper down, exposing the long line of her spine, the tiny tie of her bikini the only interruption.

I swallow.

I lower the zipper farther until it reaches the dip of her lower back, the two perfect dimples just above her pale blue bottoms. Water runs in rivulets down her back, and it's all I can do not to follow with my tongue.

I reach up to the collar, now wide across her shoulders. I know she doesn't need help now, but I ask, "Can I?" as I peel the neoprene off.

"Uh-huh," she says, breathy, glancing over her shoulder. There's no way I can hide my erection now.

I should step back. We agreed. This is exactly what I said I wouldn't do. But her bare skin flushed from the cold water and marked from her struggle and I can't stop. I lean forward and press a kiss to her shoulder blade. She tastes like salt. She inhales, but doesn't move, and I lean to kiss the other shoulder.

I drag the wetsuit down her arms, trapping her wrists against her sides. Her throaty moan makes my dick pulse. She doesn't attempt to free her hands, letting me take control. I tug lower, and it snags on her bottoms, dragging them down to reveal the curve of her ass and the most dangerous inch of skin I've ever seen.

"Fuck," I groan, my grip tightening.

"Max," she breathes and arches her back, tipping her ass toward me like an offering I can't refuse. I band my arm around her waist to pull her tight against me, slotting my erection between her ass cheeks. "Yes." She sags against me. I snake my other hand up to her throat to tip her head, exposing the long line of her neck.

I kiss the juncture where her neck meets her shoulder and lick a cascading drop of water upwards until my tongue ends at the soft spot behind her ear.

We agreed to be coworkers.

Fuck the agreement.

"You taste delicious," I whisper into the shell of her ear. Her arms are still pinned, but she pushes her ass firmer into my lap.

I hold her chin where I want it, kissing and sucking while my other hand moves up over the soft swell of her belly to cup the underside of her breast. I block the stream of water with the back of my hand as I drag my thumb over her pebbled nipple beneath the tiny triangle of her bikini. When I tug the fabric to the side, I let the water pelt her exposed nipple while I pinch and roll it between my thumb and forefinger.

She shifts against her wetsuit restraints, and I reach down to free her.

"No!" she says, tipping her head back so I can finally claim her mouth.

Her lips are still chilled from the ocean. But her mouth is warm and wet as she kisses me frantically, sucking my bottom lip between her teeth. Aside from her mouth and the way she grinds her ass against my erection, she is completely pliant. And fuck if it isn't the biggest turn on to have her let go like this, to give over her control.

I'm overwhelmed by how much I want her—but even more by how much I want her like this. Unguarded. Trusting. Choosing me without armor. I slide my hand to the ridge where her wetsuit is doubled over her lower abdomen, tight like a neoprene chastity belt.

"I want to touch you."

"I want you to touch me," she moans and sinks deeper into my grip.

I wriggle my hand between the wetsuit and her skin, still cold despite the hot shower. I move lower until I find the heat of her slick center. The neoprene keeps my hand wedged tight against her, and that's almost enough to make me come.

I can hardly move my hand, and there's no way I can plunge my fingers inside her like I so desperately want. But fuck if I'm not going to make her come like this. I begin to move my fingers in slow circles over her clit. Every other movement between us stills.

She lets her head tip back on my shoulder, her eyes closing as she pulls her lip between her teeth. A quiet whimper escapes that the shower can't drown out, settling low in my chest, heavy and warm. I turn us slightly, blocking her so the water hits my shoulder, soaking my clothes.

Without the stream of water, I can feel her arousal increase, coating my fingers, and I pick up my pace.

"Please don't stop."

"Oh, baby, I don't plan on it."

I increase my pressure and speed, my gaze locked on her face for cues I'm doing it right. It hits me all at once that this isn't about finally getting her or even just her pleasure—it's about not ruining the way she's giving herself to me.

She breaks around my fingers. Doesn't convulse or writhe like at Bar None—she just comes. And something about it feels so vulnerable, so intimate, like it's a privilege to be here, to witness her come undone.

She sags against me, spent, and I'm supporting all her weight with the arm banded around her ribcage.

I kiss her temple and slowly withdraw my hand.

She doesn't move or speak, simply wears a quiet, contented smile that makes me want to gather her into my arms and keep her there. I bunch the wetsuit in my hands, holding it taut so she can slip free.

"Let's get you out of this and dried off," I whisper. "Are you still cold?"

"No." She shakes her head and turns in my arms so I can stare into her green eyes. Her lids are heavy, satisfied, her cheeks flushed from the water or the orgasm. She cups my jaw, dragging her thumb across my lip in a way that reminds me how hard I still am.

She presses a simple kiss to my lips like a thank you, then says, "I want you to fuck me."

My grip tightens—not to stop her. Because I already know I won't.

Chapter 13

Harper

Max's grip tightens on my upper arms, and I think for a moment he's going to push me away. Instead, he backs me up, kissing me so fiercely that my head bounces against the cement wall.

"Fuck, sorry," he pulls back, cupping my face. "Are you okay?"

"Yes," I lean forward to kiss him while my hands shove at my wetsuit. He takes pity on me and drops to his knees, peeling it down my legs. I steady myself with a hand on his shoulder while he tugs the neoprene off my foot. It's comically unsexy. The shower is still spraying full blast, but we've stepped out of its direct spray. Max is fully clothed and completely drenched. My other ankle is still encased in the wetsuit, the rest dragging on the sandy, wet floor. I'm shifting around, tugging at his soaking shirt, trying to get him standing so I can pull his dick out. He's had his erection pressed into my ass for the last twenty minutes and I'm ready to do something about it.

He's still trying to free my leg when it pops out, and I almost knee him in the nose, but he blocks my leg and tips over backwards, landing hard on his ass in a puddle.

I burst out laughing, and it feels like such a relief.

He crawls back toward me, caging my hips between his hands, and places a delicate kiss just above the waistband of my bathing suit.

"Maybe we should—"

"No." I shake my head and reach out my hand, hauling him to his feet. This time, I guide him backwards to the cement ledge on the other side of the shower stall. I push his shoulder until he's sitting, gazing up at me, stunned surprise and something like awe on his face.

The elevator wasn't enough. His hands on my clit until I saw stars wasn't enough. I need more. I need the whole bag of Skittles. I need him inside me.

Even if some part of me is starting to suspect that getting him out of my system isn't possible.

Even if I'm not sure I want to anymore.

I step closer, and Max keeps his hands firmly on his thighs, like we're in the champagne room of a strip club. I reach over his head to where my bag is hanging and rummage around, producing a silver foil package.

"We're doing this," I say—too fast, because slowing down would mean thinking.

I tug the tie on my bikini bottom until the fabric drops.

A whoosh of breath leaves Max's throat, and I reach back to rid myself of my top. I think for a second about the wisdom of being naked in a public bathroom. But I'm already making questionable decisions, and I can tell by the way Max's erection is tenting his sweatpants that this won't take long.

My mouth goes dry at the thought of finally getting his impressive length inside me. I meant what I said. I want him to fuck me. Or maybe I'm going to fuck him. And that's it.

Because I've learned the hard way that wanting more is where things start to unravel.

"God, Harper," Max says, still not moving, like he doesn't have permission to touch me.

I drop into a crouch in front of him and slip the condom packet between my teeth.

"Fuck," Max exhales, his whole body shudders, and I haven't even touched him yet. But he parts his legs, giving me access.

I focus on the waistband of his sweats, untying the drawstring and reaching inside, my fingers closing around what I've been thinking about since the elevator.

"Oh," we both gasp when I wrap my hand around him.

He lets his head fall back against the wall, and I give him a few long strokes, using his slick heat to lubricate my hand.

He shifts his hips away. "It's...been a while," he admits.

I look up to offer a reassuring smile.

The vulnerability in his expression isn't embarrassment, it's honest. No bravado. Just truth. Just trust.

And it steals my breath.

I reach up and tear the condom open between my teeth, then roll it carefully over his cock. I rise and straddle his thighs, his length bobbing against his stomach. He doesn't touch me until I cup his face and kiss him. Then he finally lets his hands settle on my hips. I feel the faintest tremor beneath my palms.

"Is this still okay?" I ask, pulling back to search his face.

"God, yes," he says, his fingers digging into my flesh—unmistakably inviting.

I reach between us and guide him to my entrance, lowering myself slowly. I pause—not to tease but because he's big, and I need time to take him all the way.

He slides his hands around to cup my ass, bearing some of my weight. I lean in and kiss him, focusing on my breathing, the slight burn in my thighs, the slow, delicious stretch as I sink lower.

When he's fully seated inside me, we both still.

I rest my forehead against his shoulder. He kisses my temple. My body softens, opening more fully to him.

This isn't the first time I've had casual sex. But the way our bodies fit together, the way I can feel the steady rise and fall of his breath against my chest, it all feels more reckless than a bar bathroom or a one-night stand ever has.

Because this feels like something that might linger.

I start to move, because this energy has to go somewhere.

Max lets out a sound between a plea and a warning, his fingers digging—just this side of painful—into my ass as he controls the pace.

"Yes," I breathe into his neck as we climb together.

He meets my downward slide with a sharp upward thrust.

"More," I gasp.

His hands move to the hard line of my hip bones, holding me still while he thrusts into me with force, each thrust punctuated by a broken, breathless, "I'm—close."

My hand flies to my clit, pressing fast, urgent circles, and he swears, slamming me down one final time. His body shudders inside me as I come apart around him.

We're both shaking, and he wraps his arms around my back, pulling me tight—even though we're already as close as two people can be.

He runs his fingers slowly up and down the ridges of my spine, and somehow that feels more intimate than anything before.

"We should get to work," I say, my face still tucked into his neck.

His hand stills. I feel his inhale. His exhale.

"Yeah," he says quietly. "You're probably right."

We separate carefully. He hands me a towel, averting his eyes as I wrap it around myself, then tips his head toward the door.

"I'll meet you outside."

Part of me wants to tell him he doesn't have to wait—that I'll see him later at the office. Another part wants to tell him not to leave at all. When I can't find the words, I just nod.

He nods back and goes.

I dress with unsteady hands, pulling my sweats over my still damp, slightly sticky skin. I scoop my clothes into my bag, grab the wetsuit from the floor, pausing to pick up the discarded condom wrapper.

I stare at the silver foil like it might offer an answer I don't want to ask.

This is where wanting too much ruins everything.

And I already want too much.

I thought I could get him out of my head. Instead, he feels lodged in my chest somewhere far more dangerous.

Chapter 14
Max

"Harper texted," Milo says, glancing up from his phone. "She's meeting Spencer at the site—some city code issue."

I nod, like that explains the tightness in my chest.

After the beach, we'd walked back in silence that wasn't awkward—just careful. I'd thought about suggesting we share a ride to work. But I'd stopped myself. She wouldn't want that. Or wouldn't want to be seen walking into work—late—with me.

So I'd kissed her cheek. Told her I'd see her later.

But maybe I won't.

"I need her to approve the dishware," Jessica says, already typing, "so the order can go in. I'll send the photos again. This isn't like her."

The next day, the coffee I bring her sits on her desk until it's gone cold. She never comes in to drink it.

She messages Milo instead of me, asking for the revised projections. I send them. She replies with a thumbs-up.

She doesn't come into the office.

By day three, Milo snaps his laptop shut and announces Harper wants to hold GM interviews on-site. Permits. Delays. Always something.

"Do you want me to come?" I ask, hating how quickly the words escape. "In case there's anything I can help with."

What I don't say is that I haven't been able to focus since Ocean Beach. Three days since the ocean quieted her enough to let me in. Three days since she trusted me with her body, her control, in a way that wrecked me completely.

Three days since I realized how much I want the version of Harper who shows up when she thinks no one is looking.

And now she's avoiding me entirely.

Milo waves me off. "Nah. She's in one of her heads-down moods. Best not to get in the crossfire."

On day four, I start to wonder if she's ever coming into the office again.

I organize the interview notes. I clean up the shared drive, renaming files no one asked me to rename. I triple-check timelines that were already airtight. And I pick up my phone a thousand times, thumb hovering over her name, wanting to text *What the hell is going on?* or *Did I do something wrong?* or even *Want to go surfing again?*

Every time I put the phone face down on my desk and force myself back into whatever inane tasks I'm pretending require my full attention.

Every morning, I wait a few extra minutes in the lobby with my board, watching the stairs.

Some stupid hope that she'll come down—groggy, grumpy, in those adorably oversized sweats. That we'll walk to the beach together, boards tucked under one arm, each other's hand in the other.

But I never see her.

Occasionally, I see the guy from upstairs headed to the gym, headphones already in. He always nods hello, never says a word. One morning, Andy stumbles out to let the dog she's sitting—an elderly six-pound Pomeranian named Stanley Tucci—do his business in the front garden. Somehow, I now know the dog is blind, has three teeth, a heart murmur, and a very specific bowel schedule.

But I never see Harper.

By day seven, I've stopped waiting in the lobby. Stopped checking the stairs. Stopped expecting to see her at all.

Which is exactly when we collide.

I've just collected my mail when Harper bumps into me hard enough to knock the breath from my chest.

"Oof," she huffs, lifting her head from where she was typing furiously on her phone.

For a second, I forget how to breathe. Her eyes—deep emerald, familiar in a way that makes my chest ache—lock onto mine. Her lips are still red, still distracting, and my hands itch to cup her face and kiss her like I've been starving.

A dozen questions crowd my throat—*Are you okay? Have you been sleeping? Have you eaten anything that isn't coffee?*—but I swallow them all.

The only thing that comes out is, "Why have you been avoiding me?" I ask, willing my voice not to sound desperate.

"Avoiding you?" Harper says, genuinely baffled. "Max, the city delayed our permits. The neighbors are fighting the parklet we already installed. I forgot to approve the dishware order, so guests might be eating off paper plates for the soft open, and—" she exhales sharply "—did you forget the chef can't fucking cook?"

There's too much in my chest to sort cleanly; anger, embarrassment, something that feels a lot like concern. I know she's drowning right now. I can see it all over her face.

"I know you've been busy. I'm not trying to fix it or add more to it," I say. "I just—" I stop, recalibrate. "I need to know if I imagined all of it."

She looks away, jaw tightening. "You didn't imagine it."

A beat. She's choosing her words carefully.

"The beach was great. The shower was..." She trails off, and something unguarded flickers across her face before she shuts it down. "It was a lot. And I have too much going on to..."

She stops. Presses her fingers to her temple.

"I mean, with Blake. The permits. The opening. There are a lot of people counting on me right now." She takes a shaky breath. "That's all I can focus on."

Silence stretches between us.

"I'm sorry," she says quietly. "I need...some space to get through this."

Work, standing in for everything she doesn't want to name.

"Let me help," I say, hating how much I mean it. "You said we were a good team."

She shakes her head. "I need to think straight right now. And when I'm around you..." She stops, like she's said too much. "I just can't. Not right now."

This is how it starts. The quiet rewriting. The way emotion gets filed under 'inconvenient,' and avoidance is disguised as necessity.

Got it.

I nod once and turn to leave.

"Max, wait—"

I don't turn back. I don't trust my face to stay neutral if I do.

"It's fine, Harper," I say. "I get it."

And the worst part is I do.

Chapter 15

Harper

"Harper, dear, come in," Walter says, beckoning me into a hug. "*Wheel of Fortune* is about to start."

"I can't stay long," I say, melting into his frail embrace. "Work crisis."

And maybe a personal one.

I glance around his apartment. Books and plants, Walter's two favorite pastimes, line every surface. But I notice the dust and the overflowing garbage.

"Is Gloria still coming by?" I ask, running hot water to wash a few accumulated coffee mugs and cereal bowls. I'll take the trash out when I leave.

"Who dear?" Walter asks, settling into his recliner.

"Gloria, the woman who comes to help—" I pause. Walter does not like to admit he needs help. Maybe that's why we get along. "To visit?"

"Hum," Walter thinks. "I think so, but I don't need her to visit. She just bustles around and gets in my way."

I laugh under my breath, filling two clean bowls with carbonara, Walter's favorite dish from Luca's on the corner. I hand him a bowl and settle on the couch, already pulling out my laptop, as Ryan Seacrest tells the contestant there are no "Js" in the puzzle.

"Why would you guess J first?" Walter gestures at the TV. "That's an awful guess."

Walter armchair quarterbacks *Wheel of Fortune* every night like it's his own personal Super Bowl. "Maybe it's their grandmother's initial?" I offer.

"Bah!" Walter spoons pasta into his mouth. A little falls down his chin and lands on his shirt. He notices, hesitates. I consider helping, but I know he'll shoo me away. "So, what is this big work crisis?" he asks, giving up on the errant noodle.

"Oh," I sigh. "Some drama with the chef of our new restaurant project."

"The talent," Walter mutters. "They're always the drama."

Walter Evans spent thirty years as an entertainment attorney, behind the scenes when Bill Graham built the Fillmore into an institution. Now I watch him struggle to push himself out of his chair.

"I need to come up with a solution," I say, casually standing to be closer. "So many people are counting on this launch."

"And you hate to let anyone down," Walter says, turning back to the TV. "What is that kid doing?" he yells at the screen. "This host. He's no Pat."

"Of course, I don't want to let anyone down," I say, following Walter to the kitchen. "It's my job."

"Is it?" He turns and looks at me, and I can't tell if he's having a moment where he doesn't remember what I do, or if he's calling me out. He pulls two Diet Cokes out of the fridge and hands one to me. I never drink soda, but I always have one when Walter offers.

"You have help though, don't you?" Walter says. "You mentioned hiring someone new? Is he helping?"

I look out his kitchen window, the same view from my apartment, and Max's. Just a little higher. A slightly different perspective. I wonder if Max is home right now. "He's..." I pause. "He turned out to be more of a distraction."

Walter nods knowingly.

"You know what I learned too late?" Walter says, staring out the window. "That the work is never done. There's always another deal, another client, another case. But the people..." He trails off. "The people don't wait forever."

My throat tightens.

"I thought I was building something for my family. Turns out I was just...building." He looks at me. His eyes are clear, focused in a way they haven't been all evening. "Don't make my mistake, Harper."

Then he turns back toward the TV. "Better Late Than Never!" he shouts the puzzle's answer, shuffling back to his chair to watch the rest of his show.

I stay for another round, helping Walter guess letters, but my mind keeps drifting.

The people don't wait forever.

When I leave, I pull out my phone. My thumb hovers over Max's name.

Then I open my work email instead.

"Have we settled on a launch plan yet, Harper?" Milo asks, leaning against my doorframe.

"I'm working on it," I say, not looking up from my screen.

Milo sighs, patient in the way only Milo can be. "Listen, I think Riley—" he glances down at the folder in his hands "—Lewis is the strongest GM candidate we've interviewed. Don't you?"

"Yeah," I say absently. "She was spunky. Reminded me of you."

"I think that's a compliment," Milo hedges.

"It is." I smile, giving Milo some reassurance that I have this under control.

"Great," Milo says. "But I need to give her something more than 'Bites by Blake is opening a restaurant.'"

I lean back in my chair and scrub a hand down my face. "I know. I'm working on it. Blake's lack of skills is making this more complicated."

That's one way to put it.

Everything feels more complicated lately. My to-do list is obscene.

And all I can think about is Max.

It's been four days since I asked for space. Four days of him giving it to me. He comes into the office at nine, no extra hot cappuccino from Marco's. He simply nods when he sees me, polite and professional, then settles at his desk without a word. Exactly what I said I wanted.

So why does it feel like a loss?

And despite my best effort to focus, Walter's voice plays on a loop in my head. *The work is never done but the people won't wait forever.*

My phone buzzes on the desk, snapping me out of it.

Calendar: *Bites by Blake — Meet & Greet*

Right. This.

I should go. See Blake in his element, figure out if there's anything salvageable. Right now, all I can picture is the awful food...and Max nearly choking, his fingers brushing my thigh under the table in warning. The way we'd laughed until my stomach hurt.

"Ugh," I mutter, shoving my chair back.

"I'm going to the meet and greet," I announce, stepping out of my office. "I need to see if this kid has any redeeming qualities."

"Great idea," Milo says. "I'd come with you, but I'm waiting on reference checks. You okay by yourself?"

"Of course," I say. And then, despite myself, my eyes find Max.

He isn't looking at me. He's hunched over his keyboard, squinting at the screen like it's personally offended him.

His hair is disheveled, like he's run his hands through it one too many times.

My fingers itch to smooth it down. To walk over there and fix it. To exist in his space.

I take a breath.

Then another.

"Max," I say before I've decided to. "Can you come with me?"

He looks up.

The expression that crosses his face is surprise, hurt, and something sharper. And I feel this ache behind my ribs and I don't know if it's shame or need.

God. He's not out of my system. Not even close.

But what am I even doing here?

I asked for space. He gave it to me.

And now I'm asking him to come with me?

I know that's not all I want from him.

But he goes back to New York in a few weeks. Then what? I pretend this never existed? That I didn't feel something every time he walked into a room?

"Please," I say, my voice steady even though my chest isn't. "I'd really like you to come."

He looks back down at his desk, like he's searching for an excuse to say no.

A lump catches in my throat, and I'm desperate for him to say yes.

"Yeah," he says, but he sounds defeated. "Let me get my things."

I tap my screen to order a car. Max lingers a few steps behind me, hands in his pockets, gaze on the sidewalk.When the Waymo pulls up, he opens the door for me. I slide inside.

"Welcome to Waymo, Harper," the automated voice purrs.

Max huffs softly as he climbs in. "I still can't get over these things. They'd never survive New York."

"Too many opinions?"

"Too many middle fingers."

The car glides forward. Outside, San Francisco moves in that unhurried way that makes everything feel a little surr eal.We ride in silence for a beat.

"Listen, Harper—""Can I go first?" I ask, cutting in before I lose my nerve.

He tilts his chin. "Okay."

"I don't regret anything we've done." I swallow, staring at my hands. "I just...don't always handle the aftermath very gracefully."

"Aftermath?" His mouth curves. "Like I'm a natural disaster?"

"Well," I glance at him, "you do rock my world a little."

That earns me a real laugh. "I'll take the compliment."

We're quiet. The golden hour light out the car's window fades to twilight.

"I know I've been..." I trail off, searching for the right word. "Confusing. Hot and cold. The truth is I don't know how to do...this." I gesture vaguely between us.

"Work with someone you've hooked up with?" he finishes.

And my heart hurts that he thinks that's what's hard about this. "It's just...you're leaving soon and—" I don't finish.

He's quiet for a beat. Then nods once.The acknowledgment sits heavy between us.

"I haven't really..." He exhales, rubbing the back of his neck. "I haven't done casual. I haven't really done anything since my divorce." He winces, like he's surprised the words made it out. "And I'm not asking for anything, Harper. I just don't like feeling like...it didn't matter."

My chest tightens.

"It matters," I say immediately, turning toward him. "Max, you matter. That was never it. I just can't—" I don't say, I can't afford to want something I can't keep.

He tilts his head, studying me. "You're very good at deciding what you can and can't want."

I want to ask him what he means, or defend myself, or maybe agree, but the car slows pulling up in front of a cozy bakery in Noe Valley. There's already a line curling down the sidewalk, people buzzing with anticipation.

He gives my hand a quick squeeze. "Ready?"

He steps out before I can form a response.

Not that I have one.

The crowd is thick, and my head swims a little as we work our way inside. Someone jostles me, and Max's hand settles at the base of my spine, his other hand clearing a path through the bodies.

"Harper!" Blake calls when he sees us. "Max! I'm so glad you're here!"

He pulls me into a hug, and there's something so earnest about it that my nerves finally ease after the honest car ride over.

Blake and Max exchange a quick one-arm bro hug, Blake clocking Max's at my waist.

"This is a great turnout, Blake," I say, and I mean it.

"Yeah, have you tried a Blake Bite?" he asks, gesturing toward a woman on roller skates with mini cupcakes.

He must see the alarm on my face because he adds quickly, "Relax, I didn't make them. The bakery did. It's just my name."

"Oh," I say, reassessing. "That's...great."

"Okay, I gotta work the crowd a bit," he says, jerking his thumb over his shoulder. "I'm glad you could both make it."

Once he disappears into the throng, Max leans in. "Does he know he can't cook?"

I huff. "How does this even happen? Did the whole restaurant thing snowball before anyone stopped to think it through?"

Max's hand finds my waist again, keeping me close enough that we can speak without every wannabe internet reporter overhearing.

"Sometimes things start casually," he says. "Then they pick up speed before you realize what you've agreed to."

I glance up at him, and I'm not sure we're still talking about Blake.

"My grandma loves your videos, Blake!" a fan calls, phone held high. "Can you say hi to her?"

Blake doesn't hesitate. He steps closer, smile easy. "Of course," he says. "What's your grandma's name?"

"Sarah," the woman says. "I'm Sarah too."

Blake nods, thoughtful. "And what's your favorite thing she makes for you?"

"Arroz con pollo," she says, her voice catching. "I make it for my friends now."

"That's a good one," Blake says.

He slips an arm around her shoulders and turns the phone so they're both in frame.

"Hi, Grandma Sarah," he says into the camera. "I'm here with your granddaughter, and she was telling me about your arroz con pollo."

He pauses, like this isn't content. Like it matters.

"My grandma cooks for me too," he continues. "She used to say that when she made food, she was putting a little bit of herself into it. A little love. So when I ate, I wasn't just eating her food. I was eating her love."

The crowd has gone quiet.

"And now your granddaughter is doing the same thing," Blake says gently. "She's feeding the people she loves. That started with you. You passed that down."

He smiles at the camera, warm and certain.

"That's a pretty incredible legacy, Grandma Sarah."

"This," Max murmurs at my side, "is what he's good at. Not cooking. Connecting."

Something clicks so hard it feels physical.

"That's it," I say, turning to Max. He's already watching me. That thing happens again—the electric snap when our brains sync up.

"That's it," he agrees.

"That's our fucking solution."

Chapter 16

Max

I order the car for the ride home. Harper is tapping frantically on her phone, even as she sways slightly, exhaustion catching up to her. She just changed the entire trajectory of a failing restaurant, and somehow she still thinks it isn't enough to earn her a break.

When was the last time she ate?

I think about suggesting we stop for dinner or grab something to take back to the apartment.

But she looks spent.

And I don't want to ask for more than she's already given.

She told me she didn't regret what we'd done. That I mattered. But she didn't say she wanted more.

I have to respect that.

Even if I'm starting to think I do.

I guide her into the car, my hand hovering at her back until she's settled. By the time I slide in on the other side, her head is tipped against the seat, eyes closed.

I wonder if she's asleep when she murmurs, "So...he's better with a crowd than—"

"—food?" I finish.

She laughs softly, the sound settling low in my chest.

"He's not a chef," she says, eyes still closed. "He's a conduit."

I follow the long line of her throat, the soft hollow at her collarbone. Her breathing is slow, even.

It might look like rest. But I know better. She shuts out the world so her mind can run ahead, assembling pieces before anyone else sees the pattern. I want to remind her to breathe.

And then she does.

She inhales deeply. Then exhales, long and controlled.

I've never been so proud of something so small.

"Do you think it'll work?" she asks. "Do you think people will trust him?"

"The cooking is performative," I say. "The care is real."

I wait, and when she finally looks over at me, I add, "And he's got you behind him."

"You're awfully confident in me."

You could hang the moon if you stopped getting in your own way.

"Only when I'm right."

The car pulls over too soon. I wish for traffic. For one more red light. I like this. Just being with her.

We step out in front of the building, and I punch in the code. Inside, we slow near my apartment door, like neither of us is ready to say goodnight, but neither of us knows how to ask for more.

"Okay, well." I take a step toward my door, because boundaries matter. "Goodnight, Harper."

Her gaze flicks up the stairs, then back to me.

"Do you want to come upstairs?" she asks. Her voice is quieter now. Careful. "I could make us dinner."

"It's been a long day," I say. "You don't have to—"

"I know," she says. "I'd like to."

"I thought you said you couldn't cook?" I say, watching her slowly stir another cup of broth into the simmering pan on the stove.

"I said I *didn't* cook," she corrects, her eyes flicking over to where I'm sitting at her table. "Not that I can't."

"I should never have doubted you." I take a long sip from my beer. "Is there anything Harper Wells can't do?"

"Yeah," she scoffs. "A few things."

When we got into her apartment, I caught her quick glance seeking my approval. The space was tidy and organized, as I expected, but also cozy—lived-in. This is the one place she can let her guard down. And she doesn't let too many people in.

"So," I ask, leaning my elbows on the table. "What is this secret recipe? It smells delicious."

"Risotto," she answers, standing at the kitchen stove in bare feet, her toes a shade of red that almost perfectly matches the hue of her lipstick. "I haven't made this in years."

"Why now?"

She adds more broth, turning the burner down a little. I catch the rise and fall of her back with an inhale.

"Blake's story made me think of my grandmother...and this dish."

She's quiet for a bit, and I let the silence hang instead of rushing to fill it. Harper is like a precious flower—it's a pleasure to watch her open.

"My parents worked a lot," she goes on, returning to her steady, rhythmic stirring, the movement almost hypnotic. "So I spent a lot of time with my grandmother. She would make this for me at least once a week."

"She was cooking you her love."

The tips of her dark hair bounce with her nod. "Yeah, that landed for me." She looks out the kitchen window. It's the same view as mine, but a floor up, so all we can see is the streetlight and the tops of the trees that line the sidewalk.

"This dish is simple, but it takes a lot of time," she says. "My grandmother used to say the things that really matter always do."

"Sounds wise."

"She was. She always had these little drops of wisdom that you didn't realize were so profound until later."

We're both quiet again, but it's not awkward. It's comfortable.

"I forgot how relaxing this is," she says, bending forward to inhale from the pan.

"Why did you stop?"

She shrugs. "Somewhere along the line, cooking became one of the things I had to let go of for efficiency, I guess. At some point," her voice is softer now, "I distilled everything in my life down to its most basic necessity. It felt...cleaner."

Like anonymous bar bathroom hookups instead of real intimacy, I think, but don't say.

"What did your parents do?" I ask instead.

"My mom was a real estate agent. Still is, I guess, I don't think she'll ever retire." She takes a measured inhale that I don't miss. "My dad was a history teacher."

"My mom was a history teacher too," I say with a small laugh.

"Really?" she asks, looking over her shoulder, her eyes sparkling. "We sure have a lot of...coincidences." She turns back to the stove, and it takes everything in me to stay seated. Not to go to her and wrap my arms around her waist and kiss the dip of her shoulder.

Thirty minutes later, she sets two wide bowls of perfectly creamy risotto on the table and grates fresh parmesan over each.

She sits across from me, and I hold up my beer bottle, waiting for her to toast with me.

"To eating the love," I say, and instantly regret it when her eyes flash wide for a breath.

"To eating the love," she finally says, clinking her bottle with mine.

"This is really amazing, Harper," I say after I've shoveled three huge bites into my mouth.

"Thanks." I catch genuine relief in her voice. "I haven't made it in so long, I wasn't sure how it would turn out."

"It's perfect," I say around another full bite. "You should teach Blake to make this."

"I think we should hire a recipe developer." She spoons a bite into her mouth. "And a head chef with leadership experience."

I look up from my food and watch her slip back into Harper Wells, restaurant consultant mode. It's impressive, sexy even. But I miss the Harper who was stirring her grandmother's risotto. Is there room for both versions? Could she let her worlds occupy more than one bucket?

When we finish eating, she gets up to clear the table. This time, I follow her to the sink.

"Let me," I say, taking the dish from her and running the water. "You relax."

She lets me wash the dishes, but she doesn't leave. She leans her hip against the counter next to the sink.

"Can I ask you something?"

She looks at me, cautious. "Okay."

"Why does this matter so much to you?" I gesture vaguely. "The restaurant. Studio Mise. All of it."

She's quiet for a beat, fingers tracing the edge of the counter.

"Milo and I both faced a lot of...discrimination at our old firm, I guess," she says, after a long pause. "He'll never tell you that, but I saw it. People would laugh at him behind his back."

I think about college, about how Milo was the most genuine guy I knew. But he was holding back part of himself.

"I think he created his fun-loving persona to protect himself, you know."

I nod. I understand that impulse. Molding yourself to be what you think others want to see.

"We both took a big risk starting our own thing, and big pay cuts," she continues. "But I wanted Milo to be valued for who he is and what he contributes."

I can see the protective fire behind her eyes.

"Jessica worked with us too—she quit to come to Studio Mise with us, but we couldn't pay her what she was making. I still feel guilty about that."

"But she earns a commission, right? That's pretty unheard of in your industry."

She's quiet for a long moment. I let her be, washing the dishes, letting the warm water act as meditation.

"My parents divorced when I was in middle school," she says, unprompted. "My mom worked all the time and well..." She looks out the kitchen window. "My dad had an affair."

She shakes her head, coming back to herself.

"Jessica has a family to take care of. We didn't want her to have to work extra hours, for it to affect her family, so we built the bonus system into our budgets. Milo and I took lower salaries, but when a project does well, we all do well."

She's not driven by greed or ego.

"You're not like—" I stop before I say Melanie. Melanie was win-at-all-costs. Always had her eye on the next milestone, no matter who it impacted. Harper fights for every detail because it means something. "Most big firms," I settle on instead.

"Yeah, we wanted to do things differently," she says, but there's doubt in her voice. "I want this to be successful. For them. For Milo and Jessica. And the restaurants we represent."

She's driven by the people she cares about.

"What will you do?" she says, shifting her weight so she's a little closer. "When you go back to New York?"

"I'm not sure, honestly," I say. "I think attention spans are short there, and with my background, I can easily get hired again. It's just deciding how to put myself back in there without..."

"Losing yourself?"

I nod.

"You seem to have figured it out," she says, a little catch to her voice, and starts to move away.

"Wait," I say, hand at her hip.

She stills, and I catch her chin between my thumb and forefinger and tip her face up to kiss her, slow and careful. "Thank you for cooking for me," I murmur against her lips.

She kisses me back, but I can feel her tense.

I stop.

"Max, I don't know how—" She pulls back, sucking in a sharp inhale, but doesn't drop her hands from my chest.

"You don't know how to do this?"

"Yeah."

"Can I tell you what I think?"

She starts to bristle, but I steal another kiss.

"I think you've built your life around a set of rules and standards. It's helped you be successful," I say, my hand massaging small circles on her hip. "But I don't want to be a rule you break."

Chapter 17

Harper

"I think you rush through things under the guise of productivity," Max continues, nipping at my jaw, "but really, I think it protects you from having to feel too much."

I want to bristle. To snap back. He doesn't know me well enough to say that.

Except, maybe he does. Or maybe he recognizes something he used to be.

"We don't have to rush," he says. "Not tonight. Not with this." He kisses my temple, then murmurs against my skin, "Things that matter take time."

I smile into the warmth of his mouth when it finds mine, my hands sliding down his arms, needing more. When I reach for the waistband of his jeans, he gently stills my wrist.

"You're used to being the one who decides," he says. "The one who holds everything together."

Tears suddenly threaten, the sharp snap of emotion. I don't look away. Neither does he.

"What if," he asks, pressing kisses along my throat, "you let someone else hold you together for a while?"

My chest tightens. "I want that," I admit, my voice barely steady. I don't think I realized how much until now.

His teeth graze my shoulder, just enough to make me inhale. "What if you let me take you apart, too?"

"Yes."

He pulls back to look at me. "Give me your phone."

I blink. That was not what I expected, but I reach for it anyway, fingers clumsy as I pass it over.

He silences it and slides it into the silverware drawer, shutting it with a soft click.

"What if—" Milo calls, or Kincade has a meltdown, or the million things waiting for my attention, but Max presses a kiss to my forehead.

"Stop thinking." He places his hand over my breastbone. "No one needs you right now."

His mouth trails downward, unhurried.

"Except me."

He opens the top button of my blouse, then presses a soft kiss to my exposed collarbone, dragging his teeth lightly along the ridge. A low, spreading warmth follows the path of his mouth.

"Your mind is incredible," he says, which is an absurd thing to praise while his fingers work steadily down the rest of my buttons.

He eases my shirt from my shoulders and pauses, simply looking at me.

"Your mind is incredible," he repeats when he moves again, unbuttoning my pants and shimmying them off my hips. "But it works too hard."

He helps me out of them like he's helping me off a curb. His eyes rove over me like he's taking inventory of something he intends to remember.

He presses me gently into the seat, his hands unmistakably sure.

"Your only job tonight," he continues, "is to feel."

The relief is immediate and terrifying, like setting something heavy down and realizing how long I've been carrying it.

He lowers himself in front of me. His fingers brush my thigh, close enough that my breath catches before I can stop it.

"You're very quiet," he says. "I'm not used to you not having an opinion." The words are teasing, but there's something else underneath them. Curious. Attentive.

Because my mind isn't quiet at all. It's loud with meaning. With want. With the unfamiliar relief of not having to decide what comes next.

And I don't trust myself to explain any of that.

"I'm not used to..." I start.

"Not being in charge," he finishes gently.

I swallow and dip my chin once.

He presses a chaste kiss to my thigh, sending a shiver through me.

"How about this?" he offers. "I'll tell you what to do. You decide if you want to do it. Every time."

"Yeah," I say, my voice steady even as something inside me tilts.

"Spread your legs."

My body obeys before my mind can catch up.

"See?" He smiles. "Quick learner."

A laugh slips out of me, soft and breathless, and I start to draw my legs back together. His palms land on my knees, holding me open.

"Stay."

I still. Knees wide. Only a thin strip of black lace between us. I feel so exposed to him, but it's not my body I'm concerned with. It's my emotions, raw and unguarded.

"Let me hold this," he says.

And I know he isn't talking about my body either.

I've always been in control. I was the one who followed him into the Bar None bathroom. The one who insisted on the shower at the beach. I've held every lever of my life with a white-knuckled grip, never trusting anyone else with the weight of it.

And I'm tired.

"Okay," I say.

But what I mean is: *You can have it all.*

He settles back on his heels, placing his hands on his thighs.

"Take them off for me." His voice is lower. His eyes dip between my legs.

I hook my fingers in the waistband and close my legs to slip them off. I place the lace in his waiting palm, and he stuffs it into his back pocket. My eyes flick down to my lap and back up to his eyes, now hooded, darker.

"That's right," he nods, "please spread your legs again. Show me."

Want thrums inside me, and I can already feel the slick between my legs, but I spread them wide again.

His eyes stay locked on my face.

"Scoot to the edge of the chair."

I comply, my knees wide around his kneeling frame, and he still hasn't let his gaze drop.

"Do you want me to touch you?" he asks. "Or do you want to touch yourself?"

"Uh." The sound leaves my lungs in a whoosh.

"Oh, my mistake. I'm making all the decisions tonight, sweetheart." His lips quirk into a smirk. "Have you ever touched yourself and thought of me?"

"Yes," I admit easily. My fingers grip the chair.

"When," he asks.

"After the night in the Bar None bathroom."

I catch him shift slightly.

"The first time? Did I not leave you satisfied?"

I shake my head no, pulling my lip between my teeth. "I left in a bit of a hurry."

"I remember." His eyes finally dip, just for a beat, between my legs, then back up. "Show me."

"Are you going to watch?" I tease.

He reaches out and grabs the legs of the chair, pulling me to him in one swift motion until my bare pussy is inches from his face. "Oh, I'm going to watch. And then I'm going to see what you taste like after you get yourself close."

Every nerve ending in my body explodes.

"Touch yourself, Harper."

I lower my fingers and drag them through the heat between my legs. A moan escapes my lips, and I pick up my pace. I push tight, fast circles with all four fingers against my clit. Already feeling the tightening of my impending release.

"Whoa," Max puts his hand on my arm, and I reluctantly pause. "What happened to not rushing tonight?"

"You wanted to see what I do when you aren't around," I say, my breathing ragged.

"May I try?" he asks, looking up at me and placing my hand on my leg.

I nod.

Max slides his hands around to grip the flesh of my rear and tips me up toward him.

"I've been dying to taste you, Harper."

I lean back against the chair and watch as he makes good on his promise, dragging his tongue in one long, slow stroke up my center.

"Like a fucking dream." His words vibrate against my skin. "I'm going to do that again."

"Please," I gasp out.

And he does. He licks slowly again and again until I begin to tremble, then he pulls my clit into his mouth with a hard suck.

"Max," I exhale, "I'm going to come."

Max pulls his mouth away, and I groan.

"Remember, the best things take time," Max says calmly, looking up from between my legs. "And I think you can take more before you let go."

My breath hitches. "Max, please," I beg.

"I'll continue, but only if you can promise not to come until I tell you."

My body clenches, pulling tight at his words alone, in a way that surprises me. But I take in a deep breath like that morning in my office, willing my pulse to slow.

"There you go, sweetheart," he says, placing a gentle kiss on my inner thigh. "Ready?"

I nod. Max returns his tongue to my clit, my attention instantly snapping to the orgasm I can already feel gathering.

"Breathe," he rumbles against my flesh.

I take a deep breath, and my awareness narrows to the sensation of his tongue, wet and flat against me. The drag of him running up and down my slit. The pressure of his fingertips on my thighs.

The tension coils inside again, winding me up. I suck in a quick breath, and Max pauses again, kissing just above my pubic bone.

"Slow it down," he instructs. "I've got you."

It's easier this time. The surrender, the relief. One full breath, and I nod for him to continue.

He uses his thumbs to spread me open, wide enough that the cool air hits first, followed by the warmth of his breath. The contrast snaps through me. He takes my clit into his mouth, hard, and I arch instinctively toward him.

"Not yet, Harper," he scolds, nipping at my skin.

"Fuck," I moan, and it's almost unbearable, the way he pulls me right to the edge and then eases away. My orgasms usually climb fast and spill over all at once, sharp and efficient. This is different. Slower. Deeper. So much better.

Every time Max winds me tight, the thrum of want climbs higher. And every time he reins me back with a word or anchors me with a firm squeeze of my thigh, my body resets, only to coil tighter, ache deeper, before spinning higher the next time.

"I'm going to put two fingers inside you now," he tells me, his voice a low rasp. "You're going to want to come. But don't."

My head is tipped all the way back against the chair, but I still hear it, the soft sound of him wetting his fingers in his mouth, before I feel the featherlight pressure at my entrance. His elbow and free hand keep my knees spread, holding me open, and the exposure sends a tremor through me.

"Don't come," he reminds me as he pushes inside, unhurried. I'm slick enough that he could move faster, but he doesn't. It isn't about comfort. It's about restraint.

I inhale, tracking every inch of him as he fills me completely. I exhale when he twists his wrist, hooks his fingers, dragging them out again over the rough patch of nerves inside, slow and deliberate, before thrusting back in with more force. Stars scatter behind my closed eyes.

But I don't let go.

"You're doing so well," he praises, his pace increasing enough to make my breath hitch.

"This is...incredible," I sigh. The push and pull of tension and release is dizzying, intoxicating.

"God," he mutters, his voice breaking now, "you make me so hard."

The fracture in his control almost makes me lose mine—but then I remember I don't have to hold the reins. I don't have to decide anything at all. I let myself go slack around his fingers, surrendering to the rhythm he's set, letting him fuck me slow and deep with his hand.

"Goddammit, Harper," Max groans when he feels the moment I stop managing. "You're so fucking good. You could do this all night, couldn't you?"

"Uh-huh," I breathe, and I know it's true.

Then the deliberate press of his thumb against my clit, his fingers still buried inside me, his slow circles coiling me again.

"Fuck," he groans, barely more than a whisper, before his mouth latches back onto my swollen clit, his fingers driving into me faster, harder.

It's perfect. The pace. The pressure.

I'm lost to it until he growls, "Come now."

Then, sharper, darker. "Right fucking now."

I let everything unravel. Or maybe he pulls the thread that unravels me.

I come apart like nothing I've ever felt before. My body shudders, convulses, heat spilling over his hand as he keeps me open, keeps me there.

"Oh—fuck," he stutters, one hand slipping from my thigh as he loses his own control.

I lift my head in time to watch him unravel too.

Chapter 18

Max

"Did you send Kincade the final floor plans?" Harper asks, not looking up from her screen.

"Yep," I say, adding another line to the spreadsheet. "And the revised timeline."

"Good." She makes a note on the paper in front of her. "Can you pull the supplier list for Tucker? He needs it by three."

"Already in his inbox."

She glances over, surprised. "When did you—"

"This morning," I say. "Before I got in."

"Oh." She looks back at her screen, but I catch the small smile. "Thanks."

"No problem."

Milo walks past, coffee in hand, and grins at both of us. "You two are disgustingly efficient together."

Harper rolls her eyes. "We're working, Milo."

"I know," he says, still grinning. "It's beautiful."

It had been almost two weeks since Harper pitched her solution to Blake and Kincade. Building the restaurant around the idea Blake had been articulating all along without realizing it: food is love. I'd been in the room when Harper reframed his role as Executive Chef and Culinary Curator. Blake's shoulders visibly relaxed when she told him his real talent wasn't cooking—it was storytelling.

Blake would gather recipes and stories from his fans, handed down from parents, grandparents, aunties, and beloved neighbors—including the chicken soup his mother used to make when he was sick, the dish that had accidentally launched his TikTok career after he failed spectacularly at recreating it. The most compelling recipes would be modernized by the recipe developer Harper hired, while the head chef, Tucker—a tattooed man who went by one name—would run the kitchen day to day, ensuring the food was edible.

The core menu would feature six staple dishes—Blake's chicken soup, Milo's dad's brisket, and Harper's grandmother's risotto among them—with three rotating seasonally. Blake would visit home cooks to taste the recipes that shaped them. His first stop was already scheduled: Grandma Sarah's kitchen for her arroz con pollo.

The restaurant finally had a name.

Well Loved.

Blake was ecstatic. Kincade was relieved. Harper and I were finally working together.

And it all came from Harper's focus on what mattered—not the accolades, but the people.

I had worked hard at West Financial. I was chasing the next milestone, the next win, without ever asking why. It was prestigious. Lucrative. Impressive.

But it wasn't meaningful. And I was beginning to wonder if that was my problem all along.

It had also been two weeks since Harper cooked risotto for me. Two weeks since she came apart in her kitchen, and let me put her back together.

Despite how busy we'd been, somehow at the end of each day, we found our way to each other. Simple meals Harper practiced cooking, foot rubs on the couch after long days. And every night she handed over her control like a precious gift—and I treated it that way.

She never stayed the night. She'd get dressed quickly and slip out or push me lovingly out the door with a quick kiss. But it was enough. For now. She was letting her walls down slowly, and I could be patient.

"This always smells incredible," she says as we carry our bag full of carnitas and al pastor burritos from La Taqueria into the building one evening.

"Yeah, I'm starving." I say, heading toward my door.

"Go on inside," she says, fishing a foil wrapped burrito from the bag. "I'm just going run this up to Walter. I'll be right down."

"Or I could come with you."

She glances at me, a flicker of panic crossing her face. Then she inhales and smiles. "Yeah. Okay. Let's go."

Walter opens the door in his usual cardigan, *Wheel of Fortune* playing in the background.

"Harper, dear! And you brought your young man." He beckons us in.

Harper's cheeks flush, but I reach out my hand. "Max, sir, nice to meet you."

"La Taqueria?" Walter asks, seemingly distracted by the burrito Harper's holding.

"Your favorite. Carne asada no onions," she says, handing it over.

"This one," he says to me, shaking his head affectionately. "Takes care of everyone but herself."

"I'm learning that," I say.

He settles into his recliner, already unwrapping the foil. "You're the one who's helping with the restaurant project?"

"That's me."

"And the one who's been making her smile more," he adds, eyebrows raised.

Harper flushes. "Walter—"

"What?" He takes a bite of burrito. "I'm old, not blind. You've been lighter the past few weeks." He points his burrito at me. "That's his doing, I'd wager."

I glance at Harper. She's studying her shoes, but there's a small smile tugging at her lips.

"You're good for each other. And the good ones don't wait."

"Walter." Harper's smile falters. "We're just—"

"Working," he finishes, waving his hand, seeming agitated. "I know, I know. Just don't make my mistakes."

I wonder what mistakes Walter is talking about. And I wonder what Harper was going to say about us before Walter cut her off.

"Well," Walter says brightly, as if a switch has flipped, "this burrito isn't going to eat itself. Thank you, dear. You two go on now."

Harper kisses his cheek. "We'll see you soon, Walter."

"Bring Maxwell next time too," he says as we head to the door.

"What did he mean?" I ask as we head downstairs. "About making his mistakes?"

Harper laughs it off, but it sounds forced. "Oh, I don't know. Walter gets a little confused sometimes."

I nod and decide not to push her.

"Is the Castro still the place to be for Halloween?" I ask once we've settled in my apartment with our burritos. "It's been years since I did anything fun. I usually worked and let the people with kids take the evening off. We should go out."

"Oh, my friend Amelia and her daughter are finally coming for the weekend." She glances over at me. "She has to replace her water heater, and it's turned into a whole thing. So I told her to come here while they fix it."

"Oh, okay, that sounds fun."

"No, no. You should go out. Penelope is seven, and she's going to want to trick-or-treat and—you know, kid stuff."

"Um," I hesitate.

"Plus, we probably can't, you know."

"Harper." I try to sound casual, but her words sting. Sex with Harper is incredible, but can't she see I want more than that? "Do you think I only want to be around you when we can have sex?"

"I—no. I just mean, you probably don't want to spend your Halloween collecting candy with a seven-year-old."

She's giving me an out. Not because she doesn't want me there—but because she assumes I won't want to be.

She's not used to people showing up for her. Not used to asking for what she wants. So she decides for them first.

I could push. Tell her I'd spend Halloween doing anything if it meant being with her. But maybe I can't tell her she's worth showing up for. She has to realize it herself.

"Okay," I say, turning back to my dinner. "But bring her trick-or-treating at my apartment."

"Okay." She smiles, and it feels like a victory.

"What kind of things does Penelope like?" I ask. "What is she dressing up as?"

"Oh, you know, she's seven, she's all about slime and glitter," she says, taking another bite of her burrito. "And I'm not sure what she's dressing up as exactly, but she excitedly showed me a costume with a huge purple braid when we FaceTimed. Some demon hunter or something."

"So, it's just Penelope and Amelia?" I ask. "What about her dad?"

She sighs. "He's not really in the picture anymore, or really ever."

"I don't understand that," I say, shaking my head.

"Me either. Penelope's the best, and Amelia is incredible. When Amelia got pregnant, they bought a run-down house using all her savings for the down payment. He promised to fix it up, but after six months, he moved out. Now he'll show up every few months to promise Penelope something, then back out at the last minute. The house is killing Amelia. Something is always going wrong. I want her to sell it, but she doesn't know where else to go. I want her to move closer so I can help with Penelope, but she says Reno is Penelope's home."

"Well, I'm glad they're both coming for a visit," I say, unsure how much to push. "And we can...catch up after the weekend."

"Yeah." There's a little catch in her voice. "Sounds good."

Chapter 19
Harper

"So," Amelia says, leaning against the counter, arms crossed. "Am I finally going to meet the assistant this weekend?"

"Please don't call him that," I say, positioning the cat ears that, along with my mostly black wardrobe, have been my Halloween costume staple for years. "Thank god Milo doesn't take his HR job too seriously. I'm sure this little fling is against the employee handbook."

"Little fling? Is that what we're calling it?"

"What? It's just—" I look over my shoulder to make sure Penelope is occupied with her iPad, before mouthing S.E.X. "It's...convenient."

Amelia's eyebrow lifts.

"You made him Grandma Jacqueline's risotto."

I wave my hand. "That doesn't mean anything."

"And he's met Mr. Evans."

"He lives in the building," I argue. "They're neighbors."

"You don't introduce your 'convenient sex partner' to your eighty-year-old neighbor." She studies me for a long beat. "Why are you determined not to let this be more?"

"Because it's not," I say quickly, maybe too quickly. "He's only here until the end of the month. He told me he's not looking for a relationship. And you know I don't do relationships."

"He told you that?"

"Basically," I shrug. "He's still getting over his divorce and his job, and he's taking time to regroup."

"And let's review why you don't do relationships again?"

"It's not that I never want a relationship. I just want to be more..." I search for the word, "established in my career. So I can slow down and...be around more."

"So your husband doesn't have an affair and blame you for working too much?" she asks. "You're not your parents, hon."

"Pip hon, are you almost ready?" I call, trying to steer the conversation away from Amelia's scrutiny.

"Yup!" Penelope hops off the couch and grabs a four-foot-long purple braid from the coffee table. "Can you put this in my hair, Auntie Harper?"

"Of course." I take in her outfit—denim shorts, a vinyl cropped yellow jacket straight from Spirit Halloween. "Remind me who you are again?"

"I'm Rumi," she says seriously as I clip the braid over her tiny real one. "She's the leader of Huntrix. It's a K-pop band."

"And," she adds, lowering her voice, "they're demon hunters."

"A demon hunter?" I repeat.

"K-pop demon hunters," Amelia corrects. "It's a movie. They're all obsessed."

"Yeah, but Rumi is *half*-demon," Penelope whispers, like it's classified information. "She didn't know at first."

"Hm." I smooth her baby hairs back into place. "That sounds...complicated."

"Yeah," Penelope agrees solemnly. "But she still fights the bad ones."

I finish securing the braid. "Well, Rumi," I say, "looks like you're all set."

She beams.

"Let's pop upstairs before we head out," I add. "Mr. Evans said he'd have a treat for you."

"Mr. Evans gave me a nickel," Penelope announces as we head down the stairs, fishing the coin out of her plastic pumpkin. She turns it over in her palm, brow furrowed.

"Pip," her mother says, "it was kind of him to give you something at all."

"I know, Mama," Penelope drawls, the world's tiniest verbal eye roll. "I like it. I've never gotten a nickel trick-or-treating before. I'm going to pretend it's a magic demon-hunting nickel."

"Okay, babe," Amelia says, shaking her head with a laugh.

"I want to knock on this door," Penelope declares, pointing to my neighbor's door across the hall.

"I don't think he's home, honey," I say. "He's a doctor who helps kids in other countries."

"Oh," Amelia whispers, eyes lighting up. "Is this the neighbor where the best friend and his sister were shacking up?"

"Yes," I say, too fast. "And they were fully hooking up. They thought they were being sneaky, but Walter and I saw them going up to the roof together all the time. It was obvious to everyone else in the building that they were into each other."

"Hum," Amelia hums thoughtfully. "Neighbors hooking up. Obvious to everyone else. Not obvious to them."

"It's not the same," I say.

"What does hooking up mean?" Penelope asks, already knocking on the door.

"Nothing," Amelia says brightly, stepping in to redirect her daughter down the stairs as the door to 2A swings open.

"Trick or treat!" Penelope shouts.

"Well, hey there," Cal says, crouching eye-level with Penelope. "That's a very serious costume."

"I'm Rumi. I'm in a K-pop band." Penelope beams. "And also a demon hunter."

Cal nods like this is extremely reasonable. "Of course you are." He tilts his head. "Are you hunting a specific demon tonight, or is it more of a general patrol situation?"

Penelope's eyes go wide. "General patrol. But I have a magic nickel."

"Well," Cal says, "that's the best kind."

He holds out the bowl of full-sized candy bars and lets Penelope pick, patiently holding it steady while she deliberates.

When he looks up, his eyes snag on my best friend, and I suddenly feel like I'm intruding.

"Cal," I say, but he doesn't look at me. "This is my best friend, Amelia Cassidy. Amelia, this is Cal Rhodes."

Neither of them is listening.

"And I'm Penelope Cassidy," Penelope adds helpfully. "I have Mama's last name, not my dad's."

"Penelope," Amelia says, breaking her staring contest with Cal to snap into mom mode. "That's personal information."

"Auntie Harper just told him your last name," Penelope points out.

"I meant—" Amelia exhales, regrouping. "Can you say thank you to Doctor Rhodes?"

"Oh," Cal says easily, extending a hand. "Cal's fine."

Amelia takes it. He covers her hand briefly with his other one.

"Nice to meet you," she says.

"Likewise," he replies, holding on half a second longer than necessary before turning back to Penelope. "Keep us safe out there, Rumi."

"I will!" Penelope declares, already tugging us down the stairs.

The door clicks shut behind us.

We make it three steps before I grab Amelia's arm.

"Um. What the hell was that?"

"What?" she says. "You have nice neighbors."

"One who could not stop staring at you."

"I don't know what you're talking about," she says a little too fast.

"Oh, you absolutely do."

"I want to knock on *that* door," Penelope announces once we hit the first floor.

"He's probably already out, Pip," I say. But before I can stop her, she's knocking.

Hard.

"Trick or treat!"

Max opens the door, holding a mixing bowl filled with individual pots of glitter slime. He's dressed in cropped light-wash jeans, a pink tee, pink-tinted glasses, and a perfectly styled black wig.

"Mama," Penelope breathes, awestruck, her purple fake braid swinging. "It's Jinu."

I stare, trying to work out Max's wardrobe choice.

"Your boyfriend is dressed up as my daughter's boyfriend," Amelia murmurs under her breath.

"Rumi!" Max says gravely. "I'm glad you're here. I just got word Gwi-Ma is in the area."

"Smooth." Amelia nods in approval.

"Don't worry, Jinu!" Penelope says, giggling. "I have a magic nickel!"

Max looks to us, clearly scrambling.

"Hi," Amelia says, stepping forward and offering her hand. "You must be Max. I'm Amelia—and I've heard *so* much about you."

"Hi," Max says, glancing over at me. "It's really nice to meet you too, Amelia."

Then he bends down, extending his hand to Penelope. "And you too, Rumi."

Penelope giggles again, wearing the exact same starstruck expression her mother had upstairs. "I'm not actually Rumi," she confesses. "I'm Penelope."

"Well, Penelope," Max says solemnly, shaking her hand. "We won't tell anyone."

"Mama," Penelope turns, suddenly serious, "can Jinu come trick-or-treating with us?"

Amelia snorts. "You have to ask Auntie Harper."

"Please, Auntie Harper?" Penelope pleads.

I look up at Max, who's leaning casually against the doorframe—ridiculous in the black wig and somehow still devastatingly adorable.

"Please, Auntie Harper?" he adds, soft and hopeful.

"I mean, I say yes," Amelia says, already laughing.

"You are enjoying this entirely too much," I snap at her.

"Oh, absolutely," she agrees. "I am enjoying this immensely."

"Fine," I say, throwing my hands up. "Jinu can come." I can't help the little delighted flutter behind my sternum that Max went to so much trouble.

"Jinu!" Penelope grabs his hand without hesitation. "I want to get one pound of candy tonight."

"That's ambitious," Max says, letting her drag him toward the front door. "But I respect the goal. Welp," he calls over his shoulder, "we'd better get started, Rumi."

"I feel like we're obsolete in this equation," I chuckle, looping my arm through Amelia's.

She leans in close, her voice warm and knowing.

"Ah," she murmurs. "I think you're the whole equation, my love."

Chapter 20

Max

"I feel like we just returned from an actual demon battle," Harper sighs as we walk through the apartment's front doors hours later. "Did we win?"

Penelope hit her goal of one pound of candy, ate at least half of it while her mother wasn't looking, had a minor meltdown that she couldn't possibly walk all the way home, then immediately fell asleep on my shoulder as soon as I offered to carry her.

"Thanks for carrying her, Max," Amelia says, holding out her arms.

"Let me get you ladies upstairs," I say. "I already have her settled." Truthfully, I'm not ready to say goodnight yet.

Though taking a risk with my costume and inserting myself into their night, I think it paid off. I wanted to show Harper she could trust me with more than just her body. That I could be part of it all.

"She is out," Amelia confirms, closing the door to Harper's guest room. "All that sugar made her crash hard."

"So you knew she was sneaking candy?" I ask, amused.

"A mother always knows," Amelia says with a wink, and I catch her glance at Harper who is still standing near the entryway taking off her cat ears.

Harper's fingers linger on the headband, and when she looks up, her eyes find mine for half a second too long.

Then she looks away.

"I think we are all going to sleep like the dead tonight," Harper says, running her fingers through her hair. "Who knew trick-or-treating was so exhausting?"

"Yeah," I add. "I thought I was going to have to fight a middle schooler for a mini KitKat at that last house."

Harper laughs, soft and tired, and I catch the way she's standing. Like she's holding herself back from stepping closer.

I want to ask her to come downstairs with me.

But Amelia's right here, and Harper's already building the excuse.

"I guess we should all get to bed," Harper says, her eyes flicking to mine and away again.

"Harper," Amelia says, toeing off her shoes. "I cannot sleep with that child again. She kicks like a Brazilian soccer player. Can I sleep in your bed?"

"Oh," Harper turns to look at her best friend, something silent passing between them. "Of course, we can share."

"Except," Amelia says, drawing out the word like the thought is just occurring to her. "I had that beer with dinner, which means I'm going to snore tonight. I'd hate to keep you up."

Harper narrows her eyes. "I can sleep on the couch. I need to get up early to finish some work anyway."

"No, no." Amelia pulls her into a hug, and I can see her lips moving next to Harper's ear, but can't hear what she's saying. Then, "Go stay with Max. We'll be fine."

Harper's eyes dart to me, then back to Amelia.

"I don't want to impose—"

"Harper," I say quietly. "You wouldn't be."

"I don't usually..." she trails off, glancing at Amelia and back to me, "...stay over."

"I know," I say. Because I do. She leaves every time. Like staying would mean something she's not ready to admit. "But maybe tonight you could."

She's quiet for a long moment. I can see her weighing it. Then she takes a breath. The same kind of breath she takes before making a hard decision.

"Okay," she says softly.

"Okay, you two! Goodnight!" Amelia says, closing Harper's bedroom door behind her.

"Did I just get kicked out of my apartment?" Harper asks as we make our way down the stairs.

"I think so," I laugh, but I'm thrilled. Sex with Harper is incredible, but as I glance at the folded pajamas and small toiletry bag she's carrying, this feels more meaningful. Maybe Amelia gave her a shove, but she still came.

Once we're inside, I gesture to the bathroom, and she goes in, shutting the door behind her. I go to my bedroom and change out of my Juni costume into plaid pajama bottoms and a gray t-shirt.

A few minutes later, the bathroom door opens. Harper is wearing pajama shorts and a matching top—light blue with tiny pink hearts. Wildly out of character and absolutely perfect.

Harper stands toothbrush in hand and tips her head to invite me in. I step in and wordlessly pull my toothbrush out of the medicine cabinet.

"This is cute," I say, thumbing the collar of her top.

"Does it ruin the fantasy?" she jokes.

"Nope," I say, and I mean it.

Over and over, Harper shows me her tough exterior doesn't match who she is behind closed doors. She wears all black to work, but pastel pajamas to bed. She swears more than a sailor on calls with the restaurant contractor, but spent the evening hand in hand with Penelope while she explained, in painstaking detail, the entire plot of *KPop Demon Hunters*. And Harper wasn't half-listening; she was fully engaged, asking insightful questions as if it were the most important conversation she'd ever had.

She smiles at me in the mirror while we brush our teeth, side by side. She spits into the sink, rinses her toothbrush, puts it back in her bag, then pulls out a little pot and spreads something on her lips. I watch her finger drag over the plump arch, desperately wanting to kiss her, to taste whatever she just spread. But I love this even more. I rinse my brush, replace it in the cabinet, and bend over the sink to wash my face. When I stand up, Harper is holding out a hand towel.

We exit the bathroom, and I glance back at the living room. "I can sleep on the couch."

She looks like she's debating for a moment, but says, "No, that's silly," and walks into my room. "Which side do you sleep on?" she asks, pausing at the foot of my bed.

I don't have a side, not anymore. I usually sleep starfished in the middle. "This one." I point to the side near the door.

"Good, I like the right side," she says, walking to the far side.

We take the throw pillows off the bed and pull back the covers, like we've been doing it for twenty years.

And I really like it.

More than anything else we've done together.

Getting ready for bed with her—quiet and boring—is my favorite moment we've had.

I flick on the bedside lamp and turn off the overhead light. Harper fluffs the pillows on her side and climbs in.

"How did you know to dress up like Jinu?" she asks, turning onto her side to face me once I climb in.

"I Googled demon hunters, then went to Spirit Halloween," I say, lying on my side. "And wandered the aisles until I found a costume with a purple braid."

"Really?" she asks on a quick burst of laughter.

"Yeah," I say, sliding my arm around her waist to tuck her closer. "And the teenage store clerk confirmed this was what all the kids Penelope's age were wearing this year. So I took a risk." I slide my hand down her hip to rest on the curve of her ass just below the hem of her sleep shorts.

She threads her leg between mine. "What was your favorite Halloween costume growing up?"

"Um." I think, tracing lazy circles against her skin. "I went as Batman for four consecutive years. Until my mom begged me to pick something else."

She huffs a little laugh, her eyes sparkling. "You are kind of a broody little protector."

I squeeze my fingers into her thigh, and she rolls more into me. "What about you?"

"I had a serious goth vampire phase," she says. "I think that's when my love of a red lip started."

"I love your red lip too," I say, kissing said lips.

We kiss for a long moment, both of us content not to need more. When we finally break apart, she says, "Thank you for tonight."

"I should be apologizing," I say. "I crashed your girls' night."

"It was perfect. Penelope was feeling a little...bummed...about missing trick-or-treating with her friends from school. But I think you made up for it."

"She's a great kid."

"She is," Harper agrees. "She deserves the world. They both do."

I trace my knuckle across her cheekbone. "So do you."

She doesn't tense, doesn't pull away. She just watches me, like she's trying to process something. Then she nuzzles into my shirt, burying her face.

"Are you tired?" I ask into her hair.

She nods against my chest. I remove my hand from her ass and pull the covers around her chin.

"What are you doing?" she asks, looking up at me with almost hurt on her face.

"Letting you sleep, sweetheart," I say, kissing her forehead.

"I don't want to sleep." She hitches her leg, brushing the underside of my cock.

"You sure?" I ask, even though my dick is already on board.

"So sure," she says, and it feels like more.

I roll her onto her back, her eyes sliding shut.

"These pajamas are cute." I thumb the bottom button of the shirt. "But I'm going to take them off you."

"But can we keep talking?" Her eyes don't open, but she pulls her lip between her teeth.

I stop. Wait until she opens her eyes.

"We can just talk, Harper," I say, cupping her cheek.

"No," she says, smiling, her eyes fluttering closed again. "I want both."

"Okay." I'm glad she closed her eyes again, because I'm smiling like an idiot.

"What's your favorite color?" she asks as I undo the bottom button of her pajama top.

"It used to be blue," I say, undoing another button and bending forward to kiss the skin I've exposed above the waistband of her shorts. "But lately, it's been green."

"Ocean colors," she muses, shifting her hips.

Your eyes.

"Where is your favorite place you've ever traveled?" I ask, undoing the last button on her shirt. I peel it open and place a reverent kiss between her perfect breasts.

A flush of heat blooms across her chest.

"I haven't gone anywhere in such a long time," she says, dragging her nails through my hair. "I rack up all these credit card points, but I'm too busy to use them."

I settle my weight over her, bracing on my elbow so I can kiss her lips again. She sighs when I palm her breast.

"What about you?" she asks, arching into my touch.

"Bali, probably." I tip my head to kiss the swell of her breast. "I went on a meditation and surfing retreat after—"

I freeze.

"After your divorce?" she asks, placing her hand over mine on her chest.

"Yeah," I whisper, starting to shift off her.

"Don't stop," she tips her knee to catch me between her legs, "it's okay."

I kiss her again, and I'm not sure if it's an apology or a thank you.

"Tell me about Bali." She slides her hands down our bodies, pausing when she reaches her waistband. "Should I—?"

"Let me," I say, crawling back down her body, kissing trails down her skin. I take her hand from her waistband and place a kiss on the inside of her wrist, right over her erratic pulse, before placing it on the bed next to her.

"Bali is beautiful." I hook my fingers in her shorts and pulling them down in one fluid motion. "But quiet. Too quiet at first."

I sit back on my heels and look at her, splayed out and trusting, just waiting. I pull my shirt over my head and slip out of my pants, wanting to be as naked as her.

"Too quiet is hard," she says, our gazes locked together.

"I didn't know who I was without work," I say, leaning forward to kiss her hipbone.

"Max," she exhales when I settle my fingers between her thighs.

"Turns out, I was learning how to be still." My thumb brushes slow, grounding circles. "Breathe," I tell her. *She does.*

When she goes still beneath me, I think, *she isn't just giving up control. She's learning how to be still.*

"Sounds incredible," she says, tipping her knee wide. And I need to be closer. I lean over her for the bedside table, and she places her hand on my shoulder.

"I've been tested," she says, swallowing. "If you're comfortable."

"I am," I say without hesitation. "And I haven't been—"

"I know," she says, tugging my hips back toward her.

I press into her, slowly. And she feels unreal. She rocks her hips to make room, but she's letting me set the pace. I go slow, feeling her with nothing between us. It's so incredible, I have to breathe to keep from exploding.

She matches my inhale, eyes still closed. Just feeling.

"Bali sounds magical," she says, dragging her hands up my sides.

"I'd love to take you sometime," I say, pushing into her until there is no room left between us.

She cups my face, pulling my mouth to hers while I roll my hips again and again. And it feels like a yes.

"Max," she opens her eyes, lids heavy, "tell me when to come," she says, and it's the goddamn sexiest thing I've ever experienced.

Until I wake up the next morning with her in my arms.

Sunlight filters through the blinds, and for a moment I don't move. Don't breathe. Afraid if I shift, she'll disappear.

But she doesn't.

She's still here. Soft and warm, her hair tickling my neck, one hand curled against my chest.

The plan was always to go back. Three months in San Francisco, then return to New York. Prove I could handle it. Prove the breakdown was behind me.

But lying here with Harper in my arms, the plan feels like something I made for a different person. Someone who didn't know what he was running toward—only what he was running from.

This. This is what I want.

Every morning. For the rest of my life.

Chapter 21

Harper

"I want to run this up to Walter," I say, holding the container of risotto—I can't believe is on the menu.

We just returned from the final run-through before the restaurant's soft opening tonight. Tomorrow it opens to the public, but tonight is for investors, influencers, critics, and invited friends and family to get the buzz going.

This afternoon was like a Broadway dress rehearsal. Riley, the new GM, had all the servers practice running their stations. Tucker, the head chef and kitchen manager, conducted a final test of the menu, making sure everyone from the sous chefs to the line cooks knew their part.

I wouldn't have banked on it a month ago, but we were ready.

The week before a launch, I'm usually a raging ball of anxiety and fury. But Max somehow kept me calm while still letting me stand on my own two feet. He supported me without mansplaining. Anticipated my needs before I could voice them. Knew when to step back and let me handle things myself.

And never took it personally.

He was steady and solid.

Everything I never knew I needed.

"Okay," Max says, punching the code on his door. "Want to head back to the opening together, or do you want to go on your own?"

"Why don't you meet me upstairs?" I ask. "I'll deliver this food, then maybe...we can get ready together."

Max shifts toward me, kissing my temple. "I'd like that."

"Although we might only have time for one shower," I tease, pulling his lips to mine as he groans into my mouth.

"You'd better hurry Walter's food to him," Max says against my lips, nudging me toward the stairs without breaking contact.

When I reach the top of the stairs, Walter's door is slightly ajar.

My heart stutters.

"Mr. Evans?" My voice cracks as I knock lightly, already pushing it open. "Walter?"

No answer.

The apartment is dark, and something cold slides down my spine.

My phone is in my hand before I fully register it, thumb hovering over 9-1-1, my brain already sprinting through worst-case scenarios. CPR steps. Fall protocol. How long? How—

I flick on the light.

I don't find Walter on the floor.

What I find is worse.

The apartment is empty.

Not just *Walter-isn't-home* empty. Cleared-out empty. Gone empty.

His recliner is gone.

The plants that used to crowd the windowsill, the ones he tended with such care, are gone.

Even his ridiculously oversized TV has been removed, leaving only holes in the wall, like evidence of a life that used to be here.

My throat tightens as I scan the room, disoriented, like maybe I'd walked into the wrong apartment.

Three black garbage bags sit by the door, stuffed with clothing, unceremonious and wrong.

I rush into the kitchen.

The trash can is overflowing with crumpled crossword books, discarded pill bottles, and medical supplies I don't recognize.

Oh god.

No.

When was the last time I was here?

It's only been a few days, hasn't it? I meant to stop by last night, but menu testing ran long. The day before that...I can't remember.

We were here for Halloween. Walter smiling in his doorway when he gave Penelope the magic demon-hunting nickel.

A week ago.

What can happen in a week?

My chest heaves as I move toward the back of the apartment, as if I might find him sitting calmly in bed with one of his mystery novels, as if this is all some misunderstanding I can fix.

But the bedroom is the same.

Empty, except for a bag of linens and a few forgotten items.

My vision blurs.

"Harper?"

Max's voice comes from the front of the apartment.

Then, under his breath, "Holy shit."

"Harper!" he calls again, louder, but I can't form words. My throat is locked around panic.

He's in the room in seconds, and the moment I turn, something in me breaks loose with a heaving sob.

Max catches me like he's been waiting to.

Steady. Solid.

His arms wrap around me, his hands moving in slow, grounding circles across my back.

I let myself lean.

I bury my face in his chest. Inhale him. Warmth and musk and something painfully familiar.

"It's okay," he whispers.

And for a moment, I almost believe it.

Then reality slams back.

It's not okay. Not even a little.

"I've got you," he says again, softer, into my hair.

No.

I pull back and stumble two shaky steps away, like if I stay in his arms too long, I'll fall apart completely.

Max stays still, careful, uncertain.

My chest aches.

This is why I can't do this.

I let myself get distracted—by the restaurant, by Max, by the foolish idea that I could have it all without someone getting hurt.

"I should have—" My voice fractures.

I should have known. I should have been here. I should have—

My brain is shouting the real truth:

Walter's gone. Something happened, and I missed it.

I wipe my eyes. Get it together, Harper.

"What's going through your head right now, Harper?"

That I failed Walter.

That this is what happens when I let my guard down.

And that I don't want to be therapized right now.

"Um...hello?"

The voice is so quiet I almost miss it.

Max and I both turn.

Walter's next-door neighbor stands in the doorway, half-hidden behind the frame. He's holding one of Walter's potted plants, the vines spilling over the rim.

His expression is strained, pained, as if he's been carrying this moment around for days.

"Harper, right?" he asks.

Max straightens beside me. "I'm Max," he says, holding out a hand.

"Oh. Yeah. Um..." The man shifts the plant awkwardly to one arm so he can shake. "Eli," he says with a small nod, like he's confirming it for himself. "I live—" He glances into the hall, but doesn't finish.

"Right," Max says, saving him. "I've seen you a few mornings. I live downstairs."

Eli nods once.

My impatience snaps. I want to rage, but I'm not sure at whom.

Eli's gaze drops to the plant again. His fingers tighten around the pot.

"Mr. Evans wanted me to give this to you," he says finally, extending it toward me without stepping fully inside.

My throat constricts.

"You...you talked to him?" I manage, my voice shaking. "Before..."

I can't say the word.

Eli nods quickly.

"Before he left," he says. "Yeah."

Left?

The word hits like the floor giving out beneath me.

Max's hand reaches for my elbow, careful.

"Left," I repeat, barely audible.

"His daughter came," Eli explains. "She wanted to move him closer to her. She was worried he was alone."

"He wasn't alone," I snap, and Eli flinches.

Max's grip tightens on my arm. I twist free, and he lets his hand fall.

Eli extends the plant again. "He asked me to make sure you got this."

I can't move. Can only stare at the green spill of leaves. The living thing Walter thought to leave behind.

For me.

"I'll take it," Max says when it's clear neither Eli nor I can move.

"He said it's a pothos," Eli adds, and for the first time, his mouth tips toward something like a smile. "He said you won't be able to kill it."

A wet laugh slips out of me without permission.

The room is quiet for a beat, the heaviness hanging between us.

"Change is..." Eli says, gaze dropping again. "Hard."

I try to swallow the lump in my throat.

"But he's good, Harper," Eli says, voice steadier now. "It'll be a good move for him. He'll get to see his daughter and grandkids more."

I nod, because it's true.

Because he needed more than my increasingly infrequent visits.

Because I couldn't be everything he needed.

Not with my life. Not with my pace.

I glance up at Max, still clutching the plant, watching me with a cautious gaze.

I couldn't be everything Walter needed.

And I can't be everything Max needs either.

"All right," Eli says, thumb hooking back toward his apartment. "I'd better go."

"Thanks, man," Max says, offering his hand again.

Eli hesitates, then gives a small nod and disappears into the hall.

Max and I stare at each other, and somehow the apartment feels even emptier.

"You okay?"

No.

"Yes," I say, steeling my voice.

Max's brow creases. "It's okay to not be."

"I'm fine," I snap. "He's not dead, he moved. People do that, Max."

Max's lips part, then he closes them again, like he's choosing his next words carefully.

"You don't have to turn this into something manageable," he says softly.

"I am managing it."

"You're allowed to have emotions, Harper."

I scoff. "Right, got it."

"I just meant—"

"I know what you meant, Max," I say, turning away from the pitying look on his face. "Look, I need to get to the restaurant launch." My voice is sharper than I intend. "Everyone is going to be waiting."

My phone pings, and I fish it out of my back pocket.

"Fuck," I say when I read the message from Milo.

"What is it?" Max crosses the room in a single step, reaching for my shoulder, but I duck out of his grip.

"Blake is MIA," I say, slipping past him into the hall.

Chapter 22

Max

"Max!"

Someone calls my name the second I step into the restaurant, but it isn't Harper's voice, so I don't turn.

I scan the crowd for her instead, pulse ticking as I take in how packed the space is. Bodies shoulder-to-shoulder, laughter ricocheting off the glass, phone cameras raised, people pressed up against the bar like they've been waiting for this all week.

It's hard to find anyone in the crush. But I smile.

Good job, Harper. You did it.

"Hey, surfer boy!"

This time I turn.

Andy and Liv wave from the bar. I'd told them to stop by when I saw them yesterday. I wanted Harper to have people here—cheering for her, showing up for her.

Proof that people would.

Before everything blew up.

"Wow," Liv says, eyes sweeping the room. "This is a great turnout."

"Yeah," Andy adds, grinning. "Where's that spicy little hedgehog?"

"The what?"

"She means Harper," Liv translates, then her face brightens. "Oh—hey!"

I whip around.

Not Harper.

"Max," Liv says, shifting closer, "have you met my fiancé, Owen?"

A man works his way through the crowd toward us, tall and solid, looking slightly overwhelmed by the chaos.

"I hope it's alright I invited him," Liv adds quickly. "I know you wanted a big crowd, but..." She gestures. "I think you're covered."

"Of course," I say, distracted, still searching over shoulders. "I'm glad you're all here."

"Hey, babe," Owen says when he reaches Liv, kissing her cheek. Then he looks at me and offers a hand. "It's insane out there. I had to park all the way down by Dolores Park."

"Max," I say, shaking his hand. "Nice to meet you."

"Max is the hot surfer I told you about," Andy announces, sipping her aggressively pink cocktail.

"And," Liv cuts in with a pointed look, "he helped Harper launch this restaurant."

"Oh, I hardly—"

I catch a glimpse of dark hair. Red lips. Cutting through the crowd like she's holding the whole night together by determination and force of will.

My chest tightens.

"If you'll excuse me," I say, already stepping away. "Thank you for coming."

I don't wait for an answer.

I just follow her.

"Harper!" I call, pushing into the kitchen behind her.

"Oh, good," she says, barely glancing up. "Do you have the dessert menu reprints?"

"Harper," I say again and touch her arm. "Are you okay?"

"I will be if you have the menus." She steps back, dislodging my hand. Not aggressively, but pointedly. "And when I find Blake. If he's in some alley making out with an influencer, I'm going to wring his neck."

"The menus are already at the hostess stand," I confirm, stepping into her space. "Can we talk for a minute?"

"Max, I really don't have time." Her voice is cold, detached. "Thanks for coming, though." Like I'm some fucking plus one on a guest list.

She turns and walks deeper into the kitchen.

And I follow.

The kitchen is organized chaos. Cooks and servers move like a choreographed dance. It's amazing to watch.

Harper takes the clipboard from Tucker, in a black chef's jacket, tattooed forearms exposed, his gaze flicking between the dining room and the pass like he's tracking ten things at once. She nods and hands it back to him.

She looks at me, then back down.

And I catch it. Infinitesimal. If I hadn't been staring at her completely, I would have missed it.

It's not pain, or desperation, or even help me.

It's just: Hold this.

"Harper," I call, "wait."

She looks up again as I approach, but the mask is back in place.

"Max, I need to find Blake—"

"Stop," I say. "Just stop for a minute."

"This is my job, I can't stop."

"I know. And I'm not asking you to choose between me and your work." I take a breath. "I'm just asking you to let me in. To let me help you carry this."

"I don't need—"

"Yes, you do." It comes out harder than I mean it. "You hold everything together for everyone else. Who's holding you together?"

"I don't need to be held together." Her voice sharpens. "I've been doing this my whole life. I'm fine."

"Let me hold you," I say. "Just until you can get back to doing it yourself."

Her eyes snap to mine, and there's something raw there. Wounded.

"You don't understand," she says, her voice breaking. "If I let you hold this...I won't be able to pretend I don't need you."

The words hit like a punch.

"Then don't pretend," I say.

"I can't." She shakes her head. "Max, I can't."

"Why not?"

"There are so many people counting on me, Max. Milo. Jessica. Blake." She stops herself, swallowing hard. "And if I let myself have you, someone's going to get let down. It'll be you."

"Harper," I step toward her. "That's not true."

"I'll get wrapped up in work, and you'll feel invisible, and you'll wake up and realize I'm just like Melanie."

Tears spill over, and she doesn't wipe them away.

"Harper," I cup her jaw. "You're not Melanie. You work because you care. I've watched you. You could never let me down."

She shakes her head, like she can't believe me. "But you're leaving," she whispers. "You're going back to New York at the end of the month, and I—"

"I'm not leaving."

"No." Her face goes pale. "No, Max, you can't do that."

"Why not?"

"Because I can't give you what you need!" Her voice breaks. "My mom worked all the time. My dad had an affair. Walter spent forty years putting work first and ended up alone. I've watched what happens when people try to have both. Someone always loses."

"Harper, stop. You're not Melanie. You're not your mother. And I'm not asking you to be perfect. I'm just asking you to try."

I pull her closer to me and I feel her relax, just a little. "Your sharp edges don't scare me," I say. "I'm falling in love with you, hell, I'm in love with you. All of you. The ambitious, driven, brilliant parts and the parts that are scared and messy and don't know how to let people in. I love you."

She closes her eyes.

"Don't decide for both of us," I say. "Let me choose this. Let me choose you."

For a moment, I think she's going to say yes.

But then something shifts. I can feel it as much as see it, the fear crashing back in, washing away everything I just said. Like she heard me, but can't let herself believe it. Like she can't believe she deserves it.

"I don't think I can," she whispers. "I'm sorry."

And she walks away.

Chapter 23

Harper

I push through the door into the crisp night air and finally take a full breath.

The muffled noise of the restaurant fades behind me, replaced by the hush of the city. I stare at the closed door, waiting. Hoping.

But I'm not sure whether I'm hoping Max won't follow me...

Or hoping he does.

The seconds tick by. The door doesn't open.

He's not coming.

This is what I wanted. Space. Separation. Room to sort this out.

But the ache behind my ribs doesn't feel like relief.

It feels hollow.

I just walked away from someone who said he loved me. Someone who was willing to stay. For me.

And I told him I couldn't.

That I couldn't risk failing him.

But standing here in this empty alley, I'm not sure what I'm protecting anymore. Him? Or myself?

I startle at a sharp breath behind me. I whirl around, pulse spiking, until I see a curled shape hunched against the brick wall.

"Blake?"

He scrambles to his feet, wiping at his face with the heel of his hand.

"Thank fucking god," I exhale. "Where have you been? You need to get inside."

I turn back toward the door.

"Wait—" he says, the word breaking on a shaky breath. "I can't."

I do not have time for this. Not tonight. Not when both our reputations are riding on his ability to walk into that room and be...Blake. I turn back, voice sharp. "Blake, I need you to snap out of whatever this is and get inside."

I planned for everything. The food. The drinks. The lighting. The timing. The food can run without Blake. But the restaurant can't run without his presence.

His personality.

I did not plan for a meltdown.

His...

Or mine.

Blake stands frozen in the shadows, but even in the dim light, I can see the glassy rim of his eyes.

"We're at the finish line, Blake," I say. "All the hard work is done. All you have to do is go in there and be Bites by Blake."

"I don't know how to be him right now."

"What do you mean?" I ask, swallowing down my irritation. The ticking clock in the back of my mind.

"I didn't mean for any of this to happen," he says, staring beyond the alley. "I created this whole online image by accident, Harper. It was a joke."

He lets out a shaky breath.

"It all started because I failed. I didn't drop out of culinary school because I became an influencer," he whispers. "I got kicked out."

He flinches like admitting it hurts.

"And then I pretended it was my choice. That I didn't want that life. I built this...persona to protect myself from the part of me that couldn't do it."

Protect myself.

I know that pattern.

"You don't have to do it all," I say, quieter now. "We built this so you don't have to."

His eyes flick toward the restaurant door, toward the noise drifting out and the expectations inside.

"Milo and Riley have front-of-house handled. Tucker has the kitchen under control."

Blake lets out a watery huff.

"That guy Tucker?" he says, dragging in a ragged inhale. "He's the one who should have his own restaurant. He's got it all figured out."

"I promise you, no one has it all figured out. But you know why Tucker's kitchen runs so well?" I say. "Because he gave everyone a job. He's not in there trying to carry the whole thing himself. He trusts people to do what they're good at."

Let people help you.

God, I sound like Max.

Blake shakes his head once, like he doesn't believe trust is possible.

"I think I saw Grandma Sarah in there," I try gently. "Want to go say hi?"

"I can't."

"Okay." I nod. "We'll stay here for a minute."

I hesitate, then step closer.

"But I want you to try something with me."

His eyes flick up.

"It's something I learned...from a friend...when the stress was getting to me. It feels silly, but it works."

I reach out and take his hands. They're cold and clammy, but he grips me like a lifeline.

"Can you take a breath with me?"

"What?"

"Just try."

He hesitates, then nods.

"Close your eyes."

I wait until his flutter shut, then close mine too.

"Okay. Inhale."

I draw in a slow breath. After a beat, Blake follows.

"Good," I murmur. "Again."

He does.

And I feel my pulse steadying with his.

"You deserve to be here, Blake."

He doesn't answer, but his fingers tighten around mine.

None of this would have happened without him. Without his catalyst.

"You don't have to carry all of it," I continue. "Even if it feels like you're supposed to. You just have to do the part only you can do."

His breathing evens out, slow and shaky.

"Be the guy from the bakery," I say. "The one who really cares. The one who listens. The one who connects."

I swallow hard.

"No one can do it alone," I add. "You deserve the people who gathered around you."

"Do you really think I can do this?" he asks, voice rough.

"I do," I say, opening my eyes to find his searching mine. "And we're all here to do it with you."

Blake nods. Once. Like he's choosing it.

"Okay," he says. "I'm ready."

"Good." I let go of his hands, and we turn back toward the door.

And there, leaning against the frame, arms crossed, the dim light catching the sharp line of his cheek and the sweep of his hair, is Max—watching me like he's seen straight through every wall I've built.

His smile telling me he heard every word.

Chapter 24

Max

"How long have you been standing there?" she asks, her voice quiet.

"Long enough," I say, then turn to Blake. "Milo is hoping you'll give an opening night speech at some point tonight."

"Yeah," Blake says, nodding, almost smiling. "I can do that. I'll go find him."

I clap him on the shoulder. "Great opening night, man."

He smiles, "Thanks," as he slips past me back into the kitchen.

The door swings shut, and the quiet settles over us.

"That was quite a pep talk."

"I just told him to get back in there." She shrugs.

"You gave him permission to be human."

Her eyes close, her chin tipping down.

"Does that permission extend to you as well?"

"I'm not good at this," she says, looking up at me with tears in her lashes.

"You don't have to be," I say. "We built this so you don't have to."

She nods, her shoulders relaxing slightly.

"I thought that if I could compartmentalize everything, it would protect me." She tilts toward me, breath catching. "I did the same thing Blake did. I created a persona that couldn't be hurt. But pushing you away hurts just as much. I want to let you in. But that terrifies me."

I don't say anything. She doesn't need me to interject.

"My whole life, I watched people choose between work and love. My mom worked constantly. My dad resented her for it and had an affair." She swallows hard. "Walter worked for forty years and ended up alone. I was so scared I'd do the same thing."

"Your parents' marriage didn't fail because your mom worked," I say gently. "It failed because your dad made a choice. That's on him, not her."

She's quiet for a moment, and I see something shift in her eyes. "Maybe I've been blaming the wrong person all this time."

"I don't have it all figured out either, Harper. But I'm willing to stumble through it with you."

"Are you really not going back to New York because of me?"

"You're a big reason, Harper. I won't lie." I step closer. "But you also showed me what it's like to really care about your work. Not just grind through it. You fight for people you believe in. You care about what you're building."

She leans in, her hands reaching for mine. "I really love my job."

"I love that you love your job," I laugh. "Watching you made me realize I can work hard and care."

I pull our laced fingers to my mouth and press a kiss to her knuckle.

"I don't know exactly what's next for me. But I know it's not going back to something I never loved in the first place."

"Let's figure it out," she says. "Together."

"We have gotten to be a pretty good team," I tug her to me and slot my mouth against hers. "Maybe I should see if Milo can make my job permanent."

"Maybe a little separation is okay," she chuckles and kisses me, weaving her hands into my hair, before pulling away. "How about I give you a great letter of recommendation instead?" She smiles up at me.

"Deal," I say, laughing and kissing her again. "But yes, I also want to stay to spend more time with you."

"I want that too."

"And we're going to fight," I say. "And make up. You're going to work too late and forget to eat, and I'm going to reheat Grandma's risotto and get takeout so it's warm when you get home. I'm going to be a demon hunter with Penelope, so you and Amelia can have girl time. And I'm going to tell you when it's time to close your laptop so we can have some us time too."

"And it's going to be messy," she says, but her tone makes messy sound like a relief.

"And beautiful," I finish. "And complicated. But I want to pour myself into something that matters."

"Well," she smiles up at me. "Things that matter take time."

"And the things you love are worth the effort."

"I love you," she says, settling against my chest.

I still for a moment, but I don't need to calculate my next move with her. I just have to be honest. "I love you too."

We're quiet for a long time. No more words needed, no grand gesture, no big declaration.

We both stay.

Sounds weave out of the restaurant. I tilt my head toward the door. "Sounds like they're starting the speeches. Want to go inside?"

She shakes her head. "No, I did my part. They don't need me in there. Let's go home."

"As much as I want that," I say. "This is your big night too, I think you should celebrate with the team."

She holds out her hand. "I want both."

Epilogue: Harper

1 Week Later

"God, it's beautiful out here," Max says. We're both straddling our boards, bobbing in the calm water.

He's right. It's a perfect morning.

"It is," I say, paddling closer, not wanting us to drift too far apart. "Thank you for bringing me here."

"You're the one who cashed in all her airline miles on a last-minute trip to Bali," he says, grinning.

I shrug. "Eh, I racked up so many points, never took time off to use them."

Until now.

Until him.

"I'm glad we're here," he says, looking out over the rising sun, casting everything in gold. "I wasn't sure we were ever going to leave our hotel room..." He looks back at me and winks. "Not that I'm complaining."

Heat floods my cheeks, and it has nothing to do with the sun.

"We've been here three days," I say, trying to sound indignant.

"And we've left the room exactly twice."

"This is the third time."

"My point stands." He paddles closer, his board bumping mine. "And I stand by my life choices."

I laugh, the sound carrying across the water. "We should head in," I say. "I want to go to the beachside meditation session."

"I've created a monster," he says, laughing.

We paddle back to shore, and I'm breathless by the time we reach the sand. Not from exertion—from happiness. Contentment.

I catch my board under my arm, and Max does the same, our free hands finding each other automatically.

"Oh, I can't believe I forgot to tell you this," I say as we walk toward the resort. "I ran into Liv in the lobby before we left. She wanted me to ask if you knew anyone who might want a consulting gig at RootDown."

"I love that app," he says, his eyes lighting up.

"I know—Liv is the head UX designer. Their last launch did really well, and they might IPO later this year, but they need someone to get their finances in order."

"So I'd be helping a company whose primary goal is to help people sleep better?"

"They have a meditation app too," I add.

He stops walking, turning to face me. "Sounds perfect."

"I thought so too." I squeeze his hand. "No pressure, but...I might have already told her you'd call."

He laughs, pulling me closer. "Of course you did."

We reach the outdoor showers, and I prop my board against the side of the building.

"How would you feel if I reached out to the property manager to see if I could extend my lease?" he asks, suddenly serious.

I bite my lip. "I don't think that's a good idea."

His face falls. "Of course, I can find something somewhere else. Give us our own space?"

"No, that's not what I mean," I say quickly, my heart racing. "I think maybe...you should move into my place when your lease is up."

Silence.

"Really?"

"Really." I step closer, my stomach flipping. "If we aren't going to be working together anymore, I'd like to make it easy to see each other regularly. Even when we're both busy, I want to fall asleep next to you. Every night."

His mouth curves into a smile—the kind that makes my chest ache in the best way.

"Yeah?" he says, voice rough. "Okay, I'd like that."

He pulls me into a long kiss, his hand cupping my face, thumb brushing my cheekbone.

When we break apart, he rests his forehead against mine.

"I love you," he says softly.

"I love you too."

The words come easier every time.

We stand there, dripping saltwater, the sun climbing higher behind us.

This. This is what I want.

Every morning. For the rest of my life.

"I'm going to go take a quick shower before meditation starts," I say finally, reluctantly pulling away.

"Do you need help getting out of that wetsuit?" he asks, his voice dropping lower.

I glance around. The beach is empty except for us.

"Yes." I bite my lip and nod. "Yes, I do."

The meditation session can wait.

Thank you!

Thank you so much for reading this novella. If you liked it, please consider leaving a review on Amazon, Goodreads or your own socials. Please tag me @ajclaremontwrites.

And if you want sneak peeks, bonus chapters, and behind-the-scenes on my writing journey, subscribe to my newsletter at www.ajclaremont.com

More in the Across the Hall Series

Faking It (Out Now!)
Crashing Together (Out Now!)
Sleep On It (Fall 2026)
Off the Market (Fall 2026)

Sneak Peek!

Want more from the residents Across the Hall?

Faking It

A charming stranger turns pretend fiancé.
It was supposed to be one fake date.
They seemed to forget they're *Faking It.*

Crashing Together

Brother's best friend. Only one bed.
They promised to keep it platonic.
They lied.
Now they're *Crashing Together*.

And stay tuned for: Sleep On It

A reclusive author. A sunshine intruder.
Citywide blackout.
Just until the lights come back on.
Maybe they need to *Sleep On It.*

Acknowledgements

With each book I write, I am in awe of the community of people who rally around me to support this dream of mine. And it just keeps getting bigger.

First, always, Jen. I don't think I could do anything in this life without you by my side, nor would I want to. Yes, every book is dedicated to you.

To Erik, for believing in me, often more than I believe in myself, and for doing everything you do to keep our family running so I can "write one more chapter."

Brooke, you made this book shine. Thank you for the calls, the developmental edits, and for responding to every single text that started with "What if....." I could not have done this without you.

To my ever-growing circle of writing support friends: Meg, Stephanie, Megan, Andrea, Mary, Amy, and Meghen (wow, I know a lot of Meg-adjacent people), you all make writing a little less lonely.

Lastly, this book was deeply influenced by food blogger, critically acclaimed cookbook author, and my friend, Irvin Lin. It was the story behind your blog, Eat the Love, that inspired Harper's plan for Blake's restaurant. *"Because when you eat the food that someone makes for you, you are eating their love."* It's a concept that has stayed with me ever since you shared it over a slice of your olive oil citrus cake, and everyone who has read this story has fallen in love with it too. (Try Irvin's incredible recipes yourself; visit eatthelove.com)

I hope, in some small way, my writing is that for my readers. I hope that as you read the words that came from my heart, you are reading a little of my love for you as well.

About the author

AJ Claremont writes contemporary romance packed with flirty banter, swoony heroes, and enough spice to make you fan yourself while you read.

Her stories are full of women who are both fearless and flawed, and men who are devoted but delightfully complicated — because the best love stories are never simple.

Fueled by coffee, 90s hip hop, and an endless imagination, AJ lives in Northern California with her real-life swoony husband, their two awesome teenagers, and an ever-growing TBR stack.

Keep up with AJ at ajclaremont.com or @ajclaremontwrites on Instagram

www.ingramcontent.com/pod-product-compliance
Lightning Source LLC
La Vergne TN
LVHW090609110826
845146LV00001B/315

9798985108262